A
Harlequin
Romance

OTHER

Harlequin Romances

by FLORA KIDD

Many of these titles are available at your local bookseller, or through the Harlequin Reader Service.

For a free catalogue listing all available Harlequin Romances, send your name and address to:

HARLEQUIN READER SERVICE,
M.P.O. Box 707, Niagara Falls, N.Y. 14302
Canadian address: Stratford, Ontario, Canada.

or use order coupon at back of book.

GALLANT'S FANCY

by

FLORA KIDD

HARLEQUIN BOOKS   TORONTO
WINNIPEG

Original hard cover edition published in 1974
by Mills & Boon Limited.

© Flora Kidd 1974

SBN 373-01796-0

Harlequin edition published July 1974

Printed in Canada

1796

CHAPTER ONE

'MIRANDA BENSON, Mrs Phipps wishes to see you in her office, *now*,' announced the new office girl.

'What have you been up to, Miranda, while our backs have been turned?' queried Wendy Shaw, one of Miranda's typing colleagues.

'Phippsy only wants to see you in her office if you've done something *really* wrong,' teased June Taylor, another typist. 'Surely you haven't done anything wrong, Miranda?'

Miranda Benson's pink cheeks dimpled as she smiled at the teasing, which continued at her expense and to which she had become accustomed during her four years as a typist in the offices of Transmarine Holding Company. She had typed away diligently, day in, day out, contented to be only a small part of a big international company which had its headquarters in London, England, although its interests were spread all over the world. Only once during that time had she been called into the office of Mrs Phipps, who was the supervisor of the typing pool, and that had been three months ago. Then she had been instructed to take the place of Janet Colley, secretary to Douglas Ingram, one of Transmarine's most high-powered executives. Miss Colley had been taken ill just when her boss had been in the middle of some important negotiations concerning the purchase of property, and for a few days Miranda had known what it was like to be on the inside of one of Transmarine's 'big deals'!

Knowing that she had done nothing wrong, she removed a neatly typewritten sheet of paper from her typewriter and placed it carefully in a folder. Smoothing her already smooth dark hair which fell to her shoulders from a demure centre parting, she brushed imaginary hairs from her navy-blue, white-collared dress and, picking up her handbag, she went off to Mrs Phipps' office.

Her knock was answered by a request to enter and she opened the glass-panelled door and went inside the office.

'You wish to see me, Mrs Phipps?' she asked.

Brenda Phipps was sitting behind a wide desk and was reading a letter. Her dark hair was coiffured in the latest sleek style and she was wearing a black dress with a crisp white bow at the neckline. Dark-rimmed glasses were perched on her small straight nose. Miranda had always admired her supervisor. Brenda Phipps was the epitome of the successful woman, as far as Miranda was concerned. She ran a home as well as an office and did both perfectly. Miranda hoped that one day she too would be the mother of two delightful children, the wife of someone as kindly as George Phipps and the supervisor of a typing pool or, alternatively, the efficient secretary to a top high-powered executive.

Miranda also had other dreams, but she kept those to herself because she knew that the possibilities of them ever coming true were very remote. However, they helped to pass the time when she was travelling to and from her work, and they didn't hurt a soul.

The stray thought about her day-dreams brought colour to her cheeks and a faintly dreamy expression to her clear grey eyes. Brenda Phipps saw the colour and the expression and her rather severe face softened. How lovely to be as young as Miranda, she thought wistfully, and in love.

'Good morning, Miranda. Yes, I do wish to see you. Please sit down.'

Miranda sat down obediently on a large leather-covered chair. She sat upright with her knees together and her hands folded on her lap as Aunt Clara had taught her to do and, with her shining fall of hair, pink cheeks and clear eyes, she looked like everyone's ideal of the perfect English schoolgirl in spite of the fact that she was almost twenty-two years of age.

Brenda leaned back in her swivel chair, placed her hands together and rested her chin on her fingertips. She chose her words carefully.

'How would you like to go on a cruise to the Caribbean?'

The name Caribbean immediately brought to Miranda's mind a map of those islands situated in the tropics between North and South America; a place of magical beauty where fascinating characters from history such as Sir Francis Drake, Sir Henry Morgan and Lord Nelson had lingered during their time on earth; a place of perfect sandy beaches glittering under bright sun, edged by exotic palm trees; a place where romance might come true!

'How could I go there?' she asked practically, returning to the reality of the office.

'You could go as Doug Ingram's secretary.'

'But what about Miss Colley? Doesn't he want to take her?'

'She has had to take leave of absence. That trouble she had in the autumn has returned,' explained Brenda. 'Mr Ingram has asked for you because you were involved in the initial negotiation about the purchase of real estate on an island in the Windward group.'

'Yes, I remember. The purchase couldn't go through because Mr Ingram discovered, at the last moment, that the agreement of another person who also owns land on the island was necessary. Mr Ingram said then that he would try and find the person involved and try and persuade him to agree to the sale.'

Miranda spoke in a crisp businesslike manner which Brenda noticed with approval.

'Good. I'm glad you remember the details. You were obviously interested, and interest in the problem under discussion is essential if you're going to be a good secretary. Possibly it was your interest that recommended you to Doug Ingram. I take it you would like to go?'

'Well, yes.' Miranda was suddenly breathless and all her cool aplomb deserted her. She became an excited young woman who had just been offered the chance of a life-time.

Then she thought of Joe and her face changed.

'How long would I be away?' she asked diffidently.

'A month, six weeks, possibly longer. Is it important?' asked Brenda.

'Yes, you see, I might ... I mean I'm hoping to be married in June.'

Brenda's shrewd eyes went to Miranda's clasped hands. There was no engagement ring on the left hand.

'You're not engaged,' she murmured.

'No. There's nothing official. It's just that...' Under that bright shrewd glance Miranda's glance faltered and her voice trailed away to silence.

'I see,' said Brenda with a touch of dryness. 'Then if I were you, Miranda, I'd explain to him about this offer of a job. I'm sure he'll understand, and if he really loves you he won't want to stand in your way of promotion. This is promotion. I hope you realise that.'

'Yes, Mrs Phipps, I do. I'm very grateful for the chance to go only ...'

'Take it, or leave it and return to the typing pool, Miranda, until such time as you become just another suburban housewife. The company, as you know, has recently adopted a new policy. In future it's not going to employ married typists except on a part-time basis. On the other hand it will always be interested in employing, full-time, women who have proved themselves to be capable and efficient secretaries.'

Miranda looked into Brenda's hard hazel eyes and banished all thoughts of Joe for the time being.

'I'll take it,' she said, and had a strange feeling that she had made the most momentous decision of her life. 'What do I do next?'

'Good girl!' Brenda's smile was warm again. 'Now I'll explain what it's all about. Doug Ingram is at present in New York. He has been able to contact the person whose agreement is necessary before the estate on Fortuga can be purchased by Transmarine Holdings. He has invited this person to go on a cruise through the islands on the big luxury motor yacht which the company owns. During the cruise he wants to visit those islands where Transmarine already has hotels or is developing holiday resorts. On board the yacht there will also be members of the family who first approached us and who want to sell. The idea is, of course, to have discussion about the purchase and to make an impression and show how Transmarine can benefit an under-developed area. In asking you to accompany him as his secretary Doug Ingram has shown, in my opinion, excellent taste, for I know you will make a very good hostess.'

'Hostess?' exclaimed Miranda. 'But won't Mrs Ingram be there?'

'Zelda will be there, but she will need help because there'll be other members of the family involved; wives, sisters, daughters and sons. Now I know from watching you at your work that having to entertain such an assorted group of people won't throw you. You have, if I may say so, been extremely well trained.'

'Aunt Clara,' murmured Miranda.

'Exactly,' said Brenda with a faint smile. She knew all about Clara Benson, who taught English literature in a high school and who had taken very seriously the rearing of her brother's two children when he and his wife had unfortunately been killed while on holiday in Europe. 'But to return to this business. The motor yacht is lying at the port of San Juan in the island of Puerto Rico. Doug Ingram would like you to join it there as soon as possible. I can get you on one of the charter flights which the company runs in conjunction with the Caribbean cruises we organise. You can leave Gatwick the day after tomorrow. Do you think you could be ready by then?'

Miranda's head was whirling. Having to clothe herself on her pay as a typist had never been easy and her wardrobe was kept to the bare minimum. She didn't possess, at that time of the year, one decent summer dress, and as for swim wear and evening clothes, they were non-existent.

Interpreting her distressed expression correctly, Brenda smiled and said,

'You can have an advance of pay immediately to take care of any new clothes. I advise cotton where possible, loosely fitting to avoid prickly heat. Polyester for travelling out there. You'll find suitable things in the cruise wear department of any of the good shops. If you can't buy what you want here wait until you reach St Thomas in the Virgin Islands. Zelda Ingram says the shops there are fabulous.'

'There isn't much time,' faltered Miranda, feeling rather panicky.

'Take the rest of today off and also tomorrow. I'd prefer it if you didn't say anything to the other girls in the office. They'll know soon enough,' replied Brenda, picking up the letter she had been reading and placing it in its long envelope. She handed it across the desk.

'This is for you from Mr Ingram. In it he gives you more instructions. I must say the Gallant family sound very interesting. You met Thomas Gallant when he was here, of course.'

'Yes, I did,' said Miranda, with a touch of that old-world primness which often made her more flighty colleagues go off into gales of laughter. She had not liked the way in which Thomas Gallant had regarded her for the few times she had met him in Mr Ingram's office. For a man of fifty he had seemed far too interested in the shape of her legs as revealed by her short skirt.

'Reprobates, most of them, I should guess,' mused Brenda. 'Which is hardly surprising when one thinks that they're probably descended from some scoundrelly pirate. However, I'm quite sure you'll be able to take care of yourself.'

'I hope so.'

'Perhaps a word of warning won't go amiss. Remember, for all their English names and English accents such people

10

won't behave like Englishmen. They've lived too long in the sun,' said Brenda. 'Well, shall I go ahead and make a reservation on the plane?'

'Yes, please,' replied Miranda.

On the way home that evening, travelling on the fast electric train to Dartford in Kent, where she lived with her aunt and her younger sister, Dorothy, Miranda read for a second time the letter from Doug Ingram which Mrs Phipps had given her.

After explaining how she would be met at San Juan airport, he asked her to bring out the tapes on which he had recorded the conversations he had held with Thomas Gallant in the autumn, as well as copies of the correspondence he had held with that gentleman during the past few months.

'He's a slippery customer,' the letter continued, 'and he is now asking a higher price for his property because in order to sell it without the agreement of the owner of the other half of the estate he would have to break an old entail which says that one part cannot be disposed of without the other part.

'However, I've managed to contact the owner of the other half, Roger Gallant, Thomas's cousin. I've invited him to come on a cruise to the islands. The main aim of the operation is to persuade him to agree to the sale and, if possible, to sell his half as well.

'Since he strikes me as being a very selfish, hedonistic person with no interest in his property at all, I think we have a good chance of persuading him to sell. He is, surprisingly enough, a composer of light music and has several popular songs to his credit. These are known on both sides of the Atlantic. You may have heard them. If not find out about them and be ready to flatter him, because I have it on good authority that he is susceptible to feminine charms and it's important that we make an impression on him.'

Miranda folded the letter and put it in the envelope. It seemed to her that there wasn't much to choose between the

11

Gallant cousins. They both seemed to have a similar attitude to life and to women and she did not look forward to meeting either of them.

The train drew into Dartford station and she left it, with many other commuters, to brave the sharp teeth of the east wind which was blowing straight up the Thames estuary from the North Sea.

Coat collar turned up about her ears, Miranda hurried along suburban streets lined with semi-detached houses from which lights beamed out into the wild January night. She had lived with Aunt Clara for as long as she could remember and had known no other home and no other mother. Her father had been Aunt Clara's younger brother, a clever gifted young man who had, according to his sister, made a disastrous marriage to a young woman who had been his inferior in every way.

It mattered little to Clara Benson that her sister-in-law had been warm-hearted and generous and had loved her young husband dearly. As far as Clara was concerned, Kathryn had been highly emotional and too demonstrative, often showing her deep affection for her husband in public and not caring who saw her embrace him. Since she didn't approve of such abandoned behaviour Clara had gone to great pains to subdue any signs of it in her nieces. To a certain extent she had succeeded with Miranda, who carefully repressed any emotions she felt, and she often felt deeply and passionately, hiding them under a cool, composed façade.

Clara had not been quite so successful with Dorothy, her younger niece, who had shown signs of rebelliousness at an early age and who, during her teens, had followed all sorts of strange fashions and fads. It was possible, therefore, Miranda reasoned, that Dottie had heard of Roger Gallant and his music, whereas she, with her inclination to the more serious music, which Aunt Clara provided as part of their education, had never heard of him at all.

At last she reached the semi-detached pebble-dashed

house. The door swung open when the key turned in the lock and the dark narrow hallway welcomed her as usual with smells of lemon polish and old umbrellas.

'Is that you, Miranda?' sang out Aunt Clara from the kitchen.

'Sorry, Aunty. I had to do some shopping,' Miranda called back, as she hung her coat on the old-fashioned hall stand. 'Guess what? I'm going to the Caribbean on a cruise!'

'You're not!'

Dottie stood in the doorway of the dining room where she had been setting the table for the evening meal. Taller than Miranda, her colouring was stronger, more definite and, at twenty, her figure was much fuller and more developed than her elder sister's. Dottie looked and was what the local boys called 'a bit of a handful'.

'I am. I'm flying from Gatwick on Friday to San Juan to be Mr Ingram's secretary for a month to six weeks.'

'But what about Joe?' exclaimed Dottie.

Before Miranda could reply Aunt Clara, tall and majestic, sailed through the kitchen door. Her iron-grey hair was as usual escaping wispily from its confining chignon, giving her an appearance of being careless of how she looked, which was not true. It just happened to be very fine hair which resented being restrained.

For once she was smiling, a rare occurrence, as the girls at the school where she was a teacher could testify.

'I always knew you had it in you, Miranda,' she said in her deep resonant voice, 'and I'm glad you've the sense not to let any young whippersnapper prevent you from doing what you want. What about Joe, indeed! As if he had any right to stop you from going away!'

'If he's going to marry Mirry, he has every right,' retorted Dottie, her blue eyes flashing.

'*If* is the operative word,' snorted Aunt Clara. 'He's been talking about marriage and around marriage for nearly two years, to my knowledge. And don't call your sister by that

13

FANCY

ugly contraction of her given name. Miranda is a beautiful name, chosen by me from one of my favourite pieces of literature.'

'Joe hasn't said anything definite because he's been trying to expand the business and build it up before making any new commitment,' said Miranda gently. She was used to defending Joe's procrastination in the matter of not proposing to her and not setting a date for a wedding.

'Then he has no right even to say anything to stop you from going away. He has no say at all. In my opinion he isn't half good enough for you, Miranda, and it would be a good idea if you bided your time in this matter of marriage. Plenty of fish in the sea where the Joes of this life come from, plenty. Now come and have your meal before it gets cold.'

Supper took longer than usual because there was so much to tell about the Caribbean cruise, and Miranda was still upstairs changing her clothes when Joe called to see her as he always did on a Wednesday night. Wednesday and Saturday he had called, without fail, ever since they had first met two years ago, and it was this regular routine which had led all the neighbourhood, as well as Miranda, to believe that he was courting her with a view to marrying her.

By the time she went downstairs to the sitting room Dottie had already told him the news about the forthcoming trip to the Caribbean.

'It's a bit sudden, isn't it?' he said in his forthright fashion.

He was a stockily built young man of about twenty-eight years of age, with a thatch of dark curly hair and a fresh-complexioned face. Miranda often thought he looked quite handsome, ignoring the fact that his jaw was rather heavy and that he was already inclined to be portly. His father owned a building business and Joe had recently become a partner in the business. He was ambitious and forceful and always looking for ways in which he could improve the business.

14

'Yes, it is,' she answered, 'but it's promotion.'

He gave her a sharp under-browed glance, trying to assess her feelings about her new job.

'I can see that. They must think very highly of you to send you on a trip like that. You'd be a fool to turn it down,' he said curtly. 'It'll be good experience and might come in handy later.'

She could not help feeling disappointed. He wasn't going to propose to her after all. It meant nothing to him that she was going away for six, possibly eight, weeks.

'I might be away for nearly two months,' she said softly.

'So Dottie said. Well, that's not long. I won't say I won't miss you, I shall, but I'm pretty busy just now and will be for the next few months, so I wouldn't be seeing much of you anyway. When you come back...' He paused and her heart leapt.

'Yes? When I come back?' she said breathlessly.

'We'll know better how we feel about each other, won't we? We can look upon this as a sort of test, to see whether we can get along fine without each other. I'm not very good at this love stuff.' Joe looked suddenly embarrassed for the first time since she had known him. 'You know what I mean, Mirry?'

'Yes, I know what you mean, Joe,' she said, her voice thin and strange, but he didn't seem to notice.

'Good. I thought you would.' He sounded relieved now. 'What time will you be leaving on Friday? Maybe I can take time off to drive you to the airport and see you off.'

He would do that. He would enjoy driving herself, Dottie and Aunt Clara to the airport in his new car. With a little sigh of defeat Miranda agreed she would like to be driven by him, and the rest of the evening was spent discussing his new plans for developing the business.

It was just as well, thought Miranda, that she had the excitement of shopping during her last day in England or else she might have felt very despondent. As it was, Thursday passed by in a whirl as she ransacked shops in London for the summer clothing and shoes she required. Dotty took the day off from the florist's shop in which she worked and went with her. She enjoyed it almost as much as Miranda herself and was a great help when it came to deciding whether a dress looked suitable or not.

It was while they were having a snack lunch that Miranda remembered to ask her sister about Roger Gallant and his songs. It seemed that Dottie had because she became immediately all swoony.

'Have I heard?' she demanded. 'Oh, honestly, Mirry, he writes the most fabulous tunes, and the lyrics! Well, they're out of this world. You must have heard *Stars in the Sea*. Everyone has heard that. Even Aunt Clara once said the harmonies are interesting in that. It goes like this.' She hummed a few notes. 'Of course you're so gone on all that classical stuff you never listen to any *decent* music. Actually that song was part of the music for an American film about the Caribbean. Why do you ask? Oh, Mirry! You're not going to meet him on this trip?'

Dottie's voice rose to a squeak and people in the café turned to look at the pink cheeks and shining eyes of the girl who was bounding up and down on her chair.

'Hush, Dottie. Everyone is looking at you. What would Aunt Clara say?' chided Miranda.

'I don't care. How can you be so unmoved when you're going to meet a celebrity?'

'If he's anything like his cousin Thomas I don't particularly want to meet him. He's probably in his fifties and is fat and going to seed.'

'Oh no, he isn't. That was what was so remarkable about him. His music was such a success and he was only in his middle twenties,' contradicted Dottie seriously. 'That was six years ago. Oh, you should hear Kit Williams singing those songs. He makes shivers go down my spine!'

Dottie looked in danger of swooning again and Miranda

had an almost irresistible desire to laugh at her sister's ecstatic behaviour.

'Who on earth is Kit Williams?' she asked.

'Mirry, your ignorance appalls me,' said Dottie in a good imitation of Aunt Clara! 'Who is Kit Williams, indeed? Don't you remember he was appearing in a night-club in the West End last year? Don't you ever look at the entertainments section of the newspapers? Why, he even appeared on the telly here. He's a West Indian singer, a second Harry Belafonte. He's a rave!'

'What has he to do with Roger Gallant, apart from singing his songs?' asked Miranda, mindful of Mr Ingram's suggestion that she find out as much as she could about Roger Gallant.

'He and Roger Gallant are great friends. They come from the same island, and that song I was telling you about put them both on the road to success. You know, it's a good thing you asked me or you'd have gone out to San Juan knowing absolutely nothing, Mirry, and that would have been bad. On the way home we'll call in at Sue's house. She has a record of Kit Williams singing a selection of Roger Gallant's songs,' said Dottie. 'Then you can hear the sort of music he writes.'

Later that afternoon Miranda sat in the cramped untidy bedroom belonging to Sue Green, Dottie's best friend, and listened to the soft husky voice of Kit Williams singing *Stars in the Sea* to his own guitar accompaniment. On the single bed Sue, a plump blonde girl with round blue eyes, sprawled with Dottie. Their mouths were open and their bodies were lax as they allowed themselves to be 'sent' by the music and the voice of the singer. The words were sad, if a little sentimental, telling the story of lost love. It was the music which was different, not always going in the direction one expected it to, catching the attention with discords, unusual in that type of popular ballad. It had depth and variation. It had been composed by someone who knew about music and was not just 'a flash in the pan' tune,

17

dressed up in a plushy arrangement to sound better than it was.

While she listened Miranda turned over the sleeve of the record and read the publicity blurb. It told the story of Kit Williams and how he'd been singing in a dingy night-club in San Juan when in walked old friend Roger Gallant.

'I had this poem given to me by a girl I met in St Thomas,' Kit Williams was quoted as saying. 'I showed it to Roger and there on the bar counter, amongst the empty glasses, he composed the music for it. That night I sang it in the cabaret at the club. It was heard by Syd Newton, the film director, who was in San Juan on location for a film he was making with a Caribbean background. He came up to me and wanted to meet the composer. That's how Roger and I came to be signed up to provide the background music for the film *Caribbean Crisis*.'

The brief story didn't tell her much about Roger Gallant, but it did give a brief glimpse into another world and a different way of life. The romance of overnight success for two young men would have its appeal to the younger generation, always looking for ways to prove that a person did not have to be over thirty to be successful.

Next morning, true to his word, Joe drove her to the airport. He gave her flowers, with little thought about what she should do with them on the plane, and also a huge box of chocolates. Overcome by his generosity, Miranda could not help tears starting in her eyes when he kissed her on the cheek for the second time and asked her to write to him. It was worth going away just to hear him say pleasant platitudes and give her presents, she thought as she went down the passage to the plane, but how much happier she would have felt if he'd flung his arms around her, had beseeched her not to go and had asked her to marry him.

Excitement soon banished the tears of parting. She began to take an interest in her departure. All the passengers on the plane were going out to join the big cruise ships owned by a subsidiary company of Transmarine Holdings, which

18

used San Juan as a base for weekly and fortnightly cruises amongst the islands of the Caribbean.

Miranda found herself sitting in the middle seat of three, squashed between a plump, middle-aged woman with suspiciously blonde hair and a heavily rouged and powdered face, and an equally plump swarthy-faced man.

The blonde woman had no hesitation in introducing herself. She was Mary Mowat and she came from the Midlands.

'Much as I love my home town I'm glad to get away from it at this time of the year,' she confided in Miranda. 'If I see anything worth seeing through this window I'll let you look. It's going to be a tedious flight. Nine hours, they tell me. We may as well be friendly from the start. Are you going on the cruise too?'

Before the first hour of the flight was over Miranda had told Mrs Mowat all about her job and had heard all about Mrs Mowat's winter cruises in various warm climates. She was lively and knowledgeable, sharply witty as so many merry English widows are.

'This is my first to the Caribbean,' she said. 'I've all sorts of people to visit. I've an introduction to the Chief Justice of one of the islands and I'm going to visit the daughter of a friend of mine who lives on Grenada. She went out there with her husband in a sailing yacht. Imagine, all those miles in a little boat! Only took them six weeks. Oh, look, the cloud has cleared. I can see the ocean. Lean this way and look for yourself.'

Miranda looked and was amazed to see thousands of feet below a stretch of crushed blue satin which was the Atlantic Ocean. She could even see the shape of a ship, a small speck moving slowly across the blue.

Aperitifs were brought by the stewardesses and Miranda learned that the man on her right was Harry Walton, a London business man who was also flying out to his first Carribean cruise.

'I couldn't stand the January weather in England another

19

week,' he said, 'so I got my secretary to phone my travel agent and ask him what was available in the way of a holiday in the sun. He came up with this. Fly out to San Juan, spend two weeks cruising about the islands. And here I am with Lily—that's Lily, my wife, sitting in front. Ah, I can hardly wait to feel all that sunshine beating down on me. Now what are you going to drink? It's on the house, so make the most of it. Fruit juice? Are you sure? Rum for me. Might as well start drinking the stuff. Wait until you've been out there a few weeks. I bet you'll be downing Barbados swizzles with the best.'

There was so much happening on the plane that Miranda didn't have time to feel bored. She watched the stewardesses manoeuvre their trolleys up and down the aisle between the seats and serve everyone with a pleasant smile. They had hardly finished serving the drinks when they were back with a meal, although which meal it was supposed to be Miranda couldn't be sure since she was quite confused about the time.

When the meal was over Mrs Mowat slept and snored a little on the left and Mr Walton slept and snored a little on the right. Miranda leafed through a magazine and wondered who would be at the airport in San Juan to meet her.

Afternoon tea was served and then the captain of the aircraft spoke. It was time for them to adjust their watches as they were approaching San Juan where it was almost four in the afternoon. The weather there was thundery and rain was falling. The temperature was seventy-eight degrees Fahrenheit.

Excitement raced through Miranda. Soon she would be on foreign soil for the first time in her life. Although she had left England hours ago she had not felt as if she had left it because the plane was British and the people all around her were British. In half an hour she would be in Puerto Rico, now part of the United States, but originally founded and settled by the Spanish and where the language spoken

20

by the inhabitants was Spanish.

There was a buzz of excited conversation amongst the passengers. Mrs Mowat and Mr Walton discovered that they had mutual acquaintances. Lily Walton leaned back in her seat to speak to Miranda. Laughter and friendliness were the order of the day as a holiday mood prevailed throughout the plane.

Then Mrs Mowat was leaning back in her seat so that Miranda could see through the window. She had a view of the sea, nearer now, scattered with large white flecks which she realised with surprise were the crests of waves. In the distance, rising out of an expanse of brillant aquamarine water, was a mauve smudge—an island.

Later when she looked down it was to see the deep blue of the sea changing to emerald where it grew shallow near the pale yellow sands on which foaming breakers tumbled. Stately palm trees lifted their broad leaves as a sudden wind blew out of a purple cloud. Beyond the beach and the palms rose high white skyscrapers above flat-roofed houses and wooden shacks. Behind them was the backcloth of the hills, thickly clothed in the green vegetation, the thick rain forest of Puerto Rico. Then everything was hidden from sight by slanting rain as a tropical storm hit the town.

The plane circled lower, touched the runway, slowed down to taxi up to the airport building and stopped. Immediately there was movement as the passengers, released from their seats, stood up and began to collect coats from racks and baggage from under seats.

Miranda's first impression of San Juan was of warm air, damp with tropical rain and tangy with the smell of the sea; of the laughter and tears of happy Puerto Ricans arriving on a flight from New York as they greeted the relatives and friends who had come to meet them; of the lovely sound of the musical Spanish language all around her.

Standing beside Mrs Mowat in the airport's arrival lounge, she watched with interest more family reunions. Lovely raven-haired girls dressed in the latest American fashions, often in bizarre and exotic colours, were being kissed by ample-bosomed equally dark-haired matrons more shabbily dressed in nondescript clothes. Slim-hipped, wide-shouldered young men with luxuriant black hair and swarthy complexions, often possessing the aquiline Castilian features of Spanish conquistadors of old, with guitars slung over their shoulders, were also being greeted. A guitar, in fact, seemed to be some sort of status symbol, and one owner actually began to strum his and began to sing a love song in Spanish, much to the delight of the family and friends who had come to greet him.

Not only Puerto Ricans had come off the American plane. There were other Americans too, tourists who had come to one of their favourite resorts for a mid-winter holiday—middle-aged women with crisp coiffures and spare angular men in lightweight suits often carrying golf clubs, another type of status symbol. White seemed to be the prevalent colour in their clothing. White pants, white jackets worn with colourful printed tunics. White blazer suits braided with red or blue. White blouses, white bags, white shoes.

One of her cases arrived and was lifted off the conveyor belt by Harry Walton.

'There you are,' he said jovially. 'We're off now. We have to join the minibus which will take us to the cruise ship. Sure you'll be all right?'

'Yes, thank you. I'll be fine.'

Mary Mowat was kissing her on the cheek, much to her surprise.

'Take care, dear, and don't get lost. It's been a pleasure to travel with you, Miranda, and remember if you should go to Grenada, look up Laura Bolton. She'll be glad to see someone young like yourself from the old country.'

They left her, and for a while tears pricked her eyes again. They were her last link with home, until she met Mr Ingram, of course. She blinked the tears away, telling herself not to be sentimental and silly. Aunt Clara would scarcely approve such a display of emotion in public. After all, she had known Mary and Harry only a few hours, so they shouldn't mean all that much to her. It was just that they were home-bred, dear and familiar with their funny jokes, people she could cling to in a strange place.

Her second case arrived and she pulled it off herself, rather appalled at its weight. The crowd had thinned out now, most people having gone through the glass doors to hail cabs or to climb into one of the buses. Her next move was to find the desk where Mr Ingram had said there would be a message waiting for her. Looking round, she saw it in a corner of the big room. Picking up her cases, she staggered over to it. By the time she reached it she was perspiring freely, unused to such exertion on a warm day. She would be glad to have a long cool drink, preferably green with lots of ice in it, to be sipped through a straw.

The young man at the desk spoke English with an American accent and simply oozed Latin charm. Yes, he had a message for her from a Mr Ingram. He had unfortunately been unable to arrange for anyone to meet her. She was to take a taxi-cab to the harbour and ask there for the motor yacht *Sea Quest*. Any cab-driver would know the wharfs where the cruise ships tied up, and she would find a cab outside the main door of the airport.

Hiding her dismay at not being met and at the thought of having to give instructions to a cab-driver who might not understand her, Miranda gave the desk clerk her usual polite confident smile and stepped back right on to the foot of someone who was standing behind her.

'Oh, I'm very sorry. I hope I didn't hurt you,' she apologised sincerely, and looked up into the baffling blankness of sun-glasses. The face around the glasses was lean and masculine and lightly tanned. A well-shaped mouth curved in a faint enigmatic smile.

'You're a long way from home,' he said.

His accent was English, impeccably so, and he was dressed in casual blue denims, the sort worn by many young people and which served to make him anonymous.

Miranda could only stare at the baffling glasses and wish he would remove them.

'My guess is that you're from London, England,' he explained, and now she noticed something un-English in his speech, a slight indolent slurring of consonants and a lilting intonation which was surely West Indian.

'Yes, I am,' she replied.

Slightly confused at being spoken to in such a familiar way by a complete stranger, she turned away and prepared to pick up her cases.

'Allow me,' offered the stranger, and before she could move he had picked up her heaviest case. In his other hand he carried his own case which had many labels stuck all over it, relics of various journeys he had taken.

'I'll get a porter,' she said.

'They're all busy, as you'll see if you look around. Where are you going?'

'The harbour.'

'My own destination,' he murmured. 'We'll go together.'

As she hesitated suspiciously he smiled properly, charmingly, showing fine even white teeth. 'Come on,' he urged. 'What have you got in this case? The kitchen sink?'

Reassured by the friendliness of his smile and by the familiar English expression about kitchen sinks, Miranda smiled back, picked up her other case and hurried after him. For all his seeming indolence he moved fast.

'It's the tapes which are heavy,' she explained.

'Tapes?' he queried, looking down at her with a lift of his finely marked eyebrows.

'Yes. My boss asked me to bring them out with me.'

'Are you meeting him at the harbour?'

'Yes. We're going for a cruise to the islands.'

'Are you now?' The drawl was amused. 'And what does his wife think of that?'

'She'll be there too. It's a business cruise and not what you're thinking at all,' she replied sharply, rebuking him, but he merely smiled at her and she felt the pink colour

24

rising in her already hot cheeks.

Automatic doors opened before them and, as they stepped out into the moist air, a big car swept up to the curb and stopped. The stranger called something in Spanish to the driver, who waved and grinned, got out of the cab and came round to open the boot and help the stranger to put the cases in it.

The man in the sun-glasses opened the back door of the car.

'In you go,' he said to Miranda.

'This is very kind of you, Mr ...' she began, hesitant again.

'Think nothing of it,' he replied with new brusqueness, brushing aside her thanks. 'We may as well share a cab since we're going in the same direction. Think of it as my way of repaying the many kindnesses I've often received in London, if it helps you to accept any more easily.'

She got in and he sat down beside her and closed the door. They set off at a fast pace swinging away from the airport and out on to a narrow road lined with palm trees. The rain had stopped and the sunlight was bright and hot, almost blinding.

Opening her handbag, Miranda searched for her sunglasses, took them out and at the same time pulled out accidentally the letter written to her by Mr Ingram. It fell to the floor of the cab and her companion bent to pick it up. He read the name and address on the envelope before returning it to her.

'Miranda Benson. Is that you?' he asked.

'Yes,' she replied primly, taking the proffered letter from him and pushing it away. Perhaps now he would tell her his own name.

'Miranda,' he said slowly. 'What a strangely romantic name for an English girl. "Do you remember an inn, Miranda? And the spreading and the tedding of the straw for a bedding? The fleas that tease in the high Pyrenees, the wine that tastes of the tar?" Are you that Miranda, I won-

25

FANCY

der, a creation of Hilaire Belloc's? Or are you Shakespeare's Miranda, the passionate innocent of his play *The Tempest*? "Admired Miranda, perfect and peerless, created of every creature's best." '

He caught Miranda staring at him in astonishment and grinned, a boyish, mischievous grin which was very disarming.

'Looking at you sitting there so precisely, looking at me as if I'm the world's prime idiot, I'd have said your name was Jane or Ann, or something else simple and commonplace, because I'm sure you're not a bit romantic, but full of common sense, and that your abilities are all practical ones,' he added.

More disconcerted than ever by this speech, Miranda took refuge behind her sun-glasses, placing them on her nose carefully. From behind the protection of the concealing brown glass she studied him more closely.

At first glance, back in the airport lounge, his casual clothes, blue denim jeans and short denim battle jacket which was the uniform of so many young people had led her to believe that he was not much older than herself. Now she could see he was older, nearer to thirty, perhaps, even 'over the hill', as those whose years were less than thirty were so fond of saying.

There was also a certain elegance about him which had not been apparent immediately. This was due, in part, to the fact that under the scuffed blue jacket he was wearing a shirt and tie. True, the shirt was undone at the collar and the knot of the tie had been loosened in deference to the heat of the day, but both shirt and tie were of excellent quality and taste. His hair, which again followed the youthful trend, was not untidy or unkempt but had been trimmed and styled by a master, and was clean and well brushed. It had the glossy sheen of the skin of a chestnut, a dark reddish-brown. For the rest, good bone structure under a taut clear skin made his face one which would not be forgotten easily. She wished she could see his eyes. It was much easier to assess people if you could see their eyes. Possibly he was aware of that and that was why he kept his hidden.

'Satisfied?' he asked suddenly, and she jumped.

'About what?' she countered, her glance going to his mouth where there might be clues to his character. It was firm yet sensitive, disciplined in repose, but curving easily into a smile when he spoke.

'About me. You've been sizing me up much as that other Miranda, the admired one, must have sized up Ferdinand when he was shipwrecked on her island. She came to the conclusion that he was a spirit from another world until her father put her right and assured her that Ferdinand was all human and although "something stained with grief, that's beauty's canker, thou mightest call him a goodly person". So might I describe myself. You're quite safe. I'm not kidnapping you, just offering you a taste of island hospitality.'

'Oh. Do you live here, then?'

'Not here, nor anywhere else, permanently, at present, but I was born and brought up on an island in the Windwards.'

That would account for his accent, thought Miranda, who remembered from her geography lessons at school that many of the islands in the Windward group had been British colonies at one time and most of them were still in the Commonwealth.

The cab was careering along at an uncomfortable pace with little regard for the roughness of the surface or for the speed limit. Shabby wooden huts seemed to grow out of the land amongst a profusion of banana bush, palm trees and bushes, bearing bright pink and yellow flowers. Here and there, at the side of the road, old battered cars were parked from which Puerto Ricans were selling a variety of articles to anyone who would buy them.

When Miranda asked about them her companion replied, 'They're *revendones*, street vendors to you. They'll sell you peeled oranges, land crabs, ices, hammocks, baskets and young coconuts, the water of which is probably the most refreshing drink when you're very hot.'

They reached a junction where the road joined a new wide boulevard along which trucks, cars and blue and white buses were hurtling. There were no traffic lights and the driver of the cab took his chance, swung his vehicle to the right and spurted forward into the stream of traffic to the accompaniment of noisy horns of the traffic coming from his left. A car drew alongside, its near window down, and the passenger hurled abuse at the cab-driver, who gave back as good as he received. Astounded by such uninhibited behaviour in the middle of fast-moving traffic, Miranda glanced at her companion. He was watching and listening, that faintly enigmatic smile curving his mouth. As the other car moved forward, pursued hotly by others, the occupants of which all shouted imprecations at the cab-driver, he leaned towards the driver and spoke to him in Spanish.

'I've asked him to drive through the more residential area instead of following the fast road,' he told Miranda. 'That way you'll see more of the place. Unfortunately San Juan has been spoilt by all those high-rise buildings. In the mid-forties the Governor decided that something must be done to attract mainlanders to visit the island. A big advertising campaign was launched and luxury hotels soared skywards. Tourist traffic waxed warm and then hot. Hotels were built everywhere. Then came trouble followed by a slump. You'll see that many of the hotels are closed.'

'That's why Transmarine aren't building here,' said Miranda musingly, as she admired the old Spanish-style villas they were passing. They had wrought-iron balconies and wide verandahs overhung with brilliant purple-red flowers which she learned later were bougainvillaeas.

'Transmarine?' echoed her companion, interest lilting through his lazy voice. 'I noticed the address on your letter. What has a nice girl like you to do with a bunch of pirates like that outfit?'

A little affronted by his jeer at the company for which she worked, Miranda answered coolly:

'I work for them. I used to be in the typing pool at the head office in London, but Mr Ingram's secretary was taken ill and I took her place while he was holding the initial negotiations for the purchase of a big estate on the island of Fortuga. You may have heard of it.'

'Yes, I've heard of it.' There was a touch of dry amusement in his voice now, and she remembered belatedly that he had said he'd been born in the Windwards. Of course he would have heard of Fortuga.

'This Ingram you mention, is he the boss you're going to meet now at the harbour?' he asked casually.

'Yes. He's the executive in charge of real estate purchase in the western hemisphere. He's very clever and has pulled off some fantastic deals,' said Miranda, who was merely quoting office gossip. 'He's invited the family who own the estate on Fortuga to take a cruise with him to show them some Transmarine hotels and holiday resorts.'

'Why does he want to do that?' he asked, and again his friendly interest spurred her to confide in him. He was a pleasant companion, easy to talk to.

'Apparently the agreement of one of the members of the family is necessary before the sale of the property can go through, and Mr Ingram has invited them all so that the whole matter can be discussed in a friendly manner. Mr Ingram says that the awkward member of the family is a very selfish person who has no interest in the estate, although he owns half of it, and he never lives there. I expect it's going to rack and ruin which is a shame when it could be developed into a thriving holiday place providing jobs for local people as well as offering pleasant vacations to visitors.'

'Have you met any of the family concerned?'

'Yes—the one who wants to sell. He came to the London office in the autumn. He's very keen to see Transmarine take over.'

'I bet he is, for a price,' was the enigmatic remark, causing her to turn and look at him sharply, but he was looking out of the window, apparently having lost interest in Trans-marine.

Miranda noticed that some of the houses were now very ostentatious. They had beautifully landscaped gardens planted with many flowering shrubs, the only one of which she recognised being the poinsettias which were still bearing the red aureole of leaves around their inconspicuous yellow flowers, which gave them their other name of 'painted leaf'. Glancing down the narrow side roads, she saw briefly the sea, flashing under the sun, a brilliant blue edged by the creamy lace of foaming breakers.

The cab turned on to a main thoroughfare. There were many new buildings built of concrete, starkly white in the sunlight. Many of them showed Spanish influence in the architecture and had elegant Moorish arches and wrought-iron balconies. Suddenly to the right she noticed warm brown stone, glowing golden in the sun, quaint round-topped turrets, sloping sturdy walls.

'What's that?' she asked, delighted by this evidence of antiquity.

'Fort San Jeronimo. It's one of a series of forts built by the Spaniards to protect the port from the marauding English and French pirates. San Juan is quite old by New World standards. It's four hundred and fifty years since the conquistadors first came here,' replied her companion. Then he added quite inconsequentially:

'What are you going to do on this so-called business cruise your boss has organised?'

'Take notes, type letters and help Mrs Ingram with the entertaining.'

'And help soften up the awkward member of the family who won't agree to sell?' The question was both shrewd and suggestive, and Miranda didn't like the implication which lay behind it.

'I would know how to go about doing that,' she replied seriously. 'And I really don't think Mr Ingram would use any underhand methods.'

30

'Don't you?' There was a touch of irony in the question. 'There speaks the innocent.'

'All I'll be able to do is point out the advantages of Transmarine over any other combine which might make an offer for the property.'

'Have you ever stayed at a Transmarine hotel?'

'No, I haven't.'

'Then you don't know much about them, do you? I don't suppose, either, that you've ever given a thought to the feelings of the islanders who suffer in the long run from invasions of organisations like Transmarine, instead of being left to develop their own place in their own way.'

'But they must benefit too, through new jobs and new facilities,' argued Miranda.

'Not always in the way that they should, and that's when the trouble starts. We're coming to the old town now. Here you'll see real beauty, a little tattered and torn, but beauty nevertheless. Someone somewhere has at last decided to care for it and spend money on it.'

The cab was passing along narrow streets lined with high-walled houses which must have been built by Spanish grandees. Long graceful windows opened on to tiny wrought-iron balconies. Beautiful gates protected inner courtyards green with shrubs and sparkling with fountains. Nearer the harbour some of the buildings were damaged and tarnished, held up by scaffolding.

Then suddenly they were on a wide street beside the harbour, a wide expanse of water glittering under the sun. Big cruise ships towered above wharfs, their paintwork white and sparkling, their bright flags fluttering gaily in the trade wind.

The cab-driver turned in his street and asked in English which wharf they wanted. Miranda's companion asked her and she realised she didn't know. She admitted her ignorance and told him the name of the yacht. He repeated it to the driver, who nodded and said something in Spanish.

The cab stopped in front of a drab-looking building

where other people were alighting from cabs and minibuses.

'We'll try here,' murmured the man in sun-glasses. 'The cab-driver says he's already taken someone to your yacht and that it's on this wharf.'

He seemed cool and withdrawn now. She sensed that the friendliness with which he had approached her and had treated her had gone. She experienced a strange pang of regret that someone who had been so kind and helpful to her was going to pass out of her life very soon.

She stepped out on to the sidewalk. The sun was very hot, striking through the polyester fibre of her suit, making it cling to her skin. Her legs felt sticky within her nylon stockings, and she longed to strip everything off and dive into the tempting blue water.

Her companion produced a wallet. Crisp green dollar notes exchanged hands, then the cab drove away. A porter approached and loaded all three cases on to his trolley. Evidently the man in sun-glasses was going to escort her to the yacht.

They passed into a cool entrance hall, walked along a passage and out at the other end on to the wide wharf. A big cruise ship loomed over them. The gangways were down and people were going aboard. As they passed its stern Miranda saw the name and recognised it as the one on which Mary Mowat and the Waltons would be cruising for two weeks.

As she plodded along behind the porter and the man in sun-glasses she felt waves of tiredness washing over her. It had been a long day and she was just beginning to feel the effects of the time lag. Ahead of her the dark red hair of the stranger glinted with copper lights. He didn't seem to feel the heat and walked easily, chatting to the porter. It was kind of him to come so far with her. Most people would not have bothered.

They were near enough to the sleek motor yacht tied up behind the cruise ship for her to see its name painted in gold letters on the stern: *Sea Quest*. Underneath the name was the port of registration: Southampton. From the jack-post the Red Ensign fluttered bravely.

'Here we are,' said the man in the sun-glasses, and he pointed to the gangway. A little hesitantly Miranda stepped on to it, wondering whether the time of parting had come.

'I'll come with you,' he murmured, and she flashed him a grateful glance, which of course he couldn't see because she was wearing sun-glasses too.

She turned and went along the gangway, over the narrow strip of water which separated the hull of the sleek white yacht from the wharf. He followed her. She stepped through the open port and found herself facing two heavy glass-panelled doors. An arm reached round her from behind and one of the doors was pulled open. She went through into blessedly cool air-conditioned dimness.

It took her some time to remove her sun-glasses and to become accustomed to the dimness after the bright light of the sun outside, and so she was not aware that a young woman was waiting in the passage way until she heard a feminine voice exclaim:

'Roger! What are you doing here?'

'The same as you, I expect,' drawled a now-familiar voice. There was a hint of ice beneath its warmth. 'I'm here to discuss the future of the Gallant estate.'

Miranda whirled round, the pleated skirt of her suit flirting out. Her wide grey eyes were accusing. He had removed his sun-glasses. The eyes which met hers were a clear ice green.

'Yes, Miranda,' he said in answer to the accusation expressed in her eyes, 'I'm the awkward member of the Gallant family, the selfish one who won't sell. I'm Roger Gallant, and I'd like to introduce you to one of my cousins, Juanita Gallant de Diaz Delgado. Nita, meet Miss Miranda Benson, Ingram's secretary.'

CHAPTER TWO

MIRANDA stood still and silent trying to deal with a storm of anger which threatened to destroy her usual composure. Mixed with the anger was the most heartrending feeling of disappointment she had ever experienced, and all because the young man who had befriended her at the airport and had escorted her to the yacht had deceived her. He had deliberately withheld his name and then led her on to talk about Transmarine.

'How do you do. I'm so glad you've arrived safely. I've been watching and waiting for you. Mrs Ingram wanted to visit Luquillo beach to swim there, so Mr Ingram has taken her. He asked me to look out for you and to show you to your cabin when you arrived. How lucky that you and Roger were able to come to the yacht together.'

Juanita, for all her exotic Spanish name and looks, spoke with the same accent as Roger, impeccably English with just a slight sibilant whisper of West Indian cadence. Words poured out of her in a breathless torrent as if she were afraid she might not say everything she had to say before someone interrupted her. About twenty-three years of age, she had a sweep of midnight-dark hair, wide laughing brown eyes and chiselled Castilian features. She was wearing a sun-dress which left her shoulders and back bare. It was white splashed with vivid colours which glowed in the dimness of the passageway.

With a great effort Miranda smiled and thanked her.

'It was no trouble,' replied the pretty, golden-skinned young woman. Then, turning to her cousin, she said, 'It's a long time since we were all together in one place like this, Roger.'

'All?' he queried drily. 'Is Marnie here?'

34

Juanita looked discomfited and the laughter fled from her eyes.

'I'd forgotten about Marnie,' she admitted in a low voice.

'Most of you do forget her all the time,' was the sharp rejoinder, and glancing at Roger quickly Miranda realised that he was as angry as she was. Anger simmered in his eyes and tautened his well-shaped mouth. 'Just because she can't see there's no reason why Marnie shouldn't be here,' he continued. 'After all, any sale of the estate affects her immediately. Did you know that Tom hadn't told her of his desire to sell his property? He hadn't told me either.'

'Then how do you know?' asked Juanita.

The simmering green glance was directed at Miranda.

'I learned on my way here. Miss Benson told me,' he said curtly.

Miranda felt limp. If there had been a wall nearby she would have sagged against it. It took all her supply of inherent English nonchalance in the face of difficulties to appear as if nothing unusual had happened and to return his gaze coolly. She had not handled the awkward Roger Gallant at all well and, even before she had begun her new job, she had managed to foul everything up.

'But if you didn't know why the cruise has been arranged why have you come? Who invited you?' asked Juanita, who was genuinely puzzled.

'Kit Williams introduced me to Ingram at a party in New York. Ingram said he was organising this cruise through the islands. He said he'd like to call at Fortuga, and would I come along for the ride. Having nothing better to do I accepted the invitation. I'd no idea that he worked for Transmarine or that his company was interested in buying the estate. If I had known you can depend upon it I would never have come. How long has this negotiating been going on, Nita? Do you know?'

'All I know is that Father went to London last fall to see Transmarine. He'd been sounding out various hotel and resort developers with a view to selling the Folly for some time. Transmarine came up with the best offer. Then Mr Ingram discovered that the Folly can't be sold without the Fancy. I suppose that's why he contacted you.'

'I see,' murmured Roger. 'And he very cleverly duped me into coming here. Why does Tom want to sell?'

'I think he's in financial trouble,' replied Juanita in a shamed voice. 'Please don't be angry, Roger. You know what he's like.'

'Only too well,' muttered Roger bitterly. 'Is Ramon with you?'

'Oh yes,' Juanita's face lit up with laughter again. 'And we've so much to tell you. We're expecting a child in June.'

A faint rather tired smile flickered across Roger's lean face.

'Good for you,' he said. 'I think you'd better do as Ingram said and take his secretary to her cabin. Presumably there's someone who can carry her cases there. Where can I get a drink?'

'There's a bar on the sun-deck. This yacht is fabulous, Roger. It has everything,' said Juanita.

'Trust Transmarine to have everything,' he remarked sardonically, with another cold glance in Miranda's direction.

Turning away, he loped up a flight of carpeted steps which led up to the next deck. Miranda watched him disappear with a mixture of relief and regret, and sagged visibly.

'You must be very tired,' Juanita sounded sympathetic and her brown eyes were anxious as she surveyed Miranda. 'I know only too well what that long flight from England is like. I used to go to school there.'

She mentioned the name of a select girls' public school in the West of England and asked if Miranda knew it. Miranda replied that she had heard of it, but forbore to mention that such a school was a far cry from the comprehensive school where she had obtained her own schooling.

'Come this way,' said Juanita, who was clearly accus-

36

tomed to commanding other people. 'Your cabin is quite
near to ours. My brother will bring your cases later. If I
were you I'd have a shower and then lie down to sleep while
you can. When the others come back from Luquillo we're
all going out to dinner and then on to a night-club to see
some flamenco dancing. Ramon, my husband, is a Puerto
Rican. His family took over the Gallant distillery a few
years ago—they're a big name in rum. I hope Roger will
come with us to the club. It's the one where he wrote the
music for *Stars in the Sea*. Did you know he's a composer
of music?'

Juanita stopped talking, presumably out of breath after
walking down another flight of carpeted steps to the lower
deck into a wide passage similar to the one they had just
left and which ran across the yacht from one side deck to
the other.

'Mr Ingram told me,' replied Miranda, unable to keep a
certain coolness from her voice.

Juanita turned to look at her.

'You *are* upset,' she murmured. 'Roger wasn't very nice.
He was angry. He isn't often angry, or if he is he doesn't
often show it. Not like me. When I'm angry you'll know
about it!' Juanita laughed in charming self-mockery. 'I
hope Roger doesn't leave. My father has been trying for
ages to meet him to discuss the future of the Gallant estate,
but Roger never answers letters. He's a very elusive person
and has always hated anything to do with business. He
cares only for music. He can be quite vague and absent-
minded at times, which is terribly irritating for the rest of
us. This way.'

She turned off down a narrow passage along the side of
the yacht. Miranda followed her, suddenly very concerned
about her own immediate future.

'I hope he doesn't leave too,' she said. 'You see, it's my
fault he knows why he was invited to come on the cruise
and if he leaves before Mr Ingram returns to the yacht I
shall be in trouble. Your cousin offered to share a cab with

37

FANCY

me because we were both coming to the harbour, and during the conversation I told him why I was here and why Mr Ingram had invited everyone. But I didn't know who he was. How could I know him?'

Juanita stopped outside a narrow door and glanced gravely at Miranda.

'You might have recognised him from a picture you might have seen,' she suggested, 'although I must admit that in those clothes and wearing dark glasses he would be hard to identify in a crowd, which is why he wore them, I expect.'

'I've never seen a picture of him. I hadn't heard of him or his music until the day before yesterday,' said Miranda with a touch of exasperation.

'Hadn't you really?' Juanita's eyes sparkled with amusement. 'Oh, he would like that. He's a very private person and he hates all the publicity that appears in connection with his songs. That's why I'm afraid he won't come to the night-club with us tonight. Luiz Benitz who owns the club might make a fuss of him and draw attention to him. What's the worst that could happen to you if he leaves before Doug Ingram comes back?'

'I might lose my job, and to tell you the truth I haven't really started it yet.'

The dark eyes softened with sympathy again and a hand squeezed her arm comfortingly.

'Don't worry. I won't let that happen. Now this is your cabin here.'

Juanita opened the door and they entered a small neatly arranged cabin which contained two single divan beds, a chest of drawers, a hanging wardrobe and a closet containing a wash basin and shower. Light came into the room through two portholes.

'Ramon and I are two doors away. It's very jolly, don't you think? There is even a radio for you.'

'Señora——' began Miranda, who was not sure by which

38

of her companion's many surnames she should address her.

'Please call me Nita,' interrupted Juanita laughingly. 'Señora is too formal and Spanish for use between two English girls. Even though I look like my Puerto Rican mother and have a Latin temperament you must always remember I was educated in England and I'm very much Thomas Gallant's daughter.'

'But surely Mrs Gallant can't be your mother!' exclaimed Miranda, recalling Dawn Gallant's silver-gilt beauty gleaming like pale sunshine in the darkness of a London office on a November afternoon.

'Dawn is my stepmother. She is only six years older than I. Father met her in Miami. She was singing with a group in a cabaret there. When she met Roger she fell in love with him, but he was looking in another direction at the time, so she settled for my father.' Juanita grimaced ruefully in self-mockery. 'I talk too much and I can see you're far too tired to be bothered with the complexities of the Gallant family. I'll find my brother Carlos, who for all his Spanish name is just like any other American undergraduate, having received his education in the States. Actually we call him Chuck, at his request. He'll bring your cases.'

She went out, and the cabin seemed extraordinarily quiet without her colourful vibrant presence.

Sighing wearily, Miranda sank down on one of the divans and kicked off her shoes. Her feet felt several sizes larger than usual. Looking at herself in the mirror she was surprised to see that she still appeared cool and collected. Her blue and white crimplene suit was still crisp and her hair was still smooth. The only signs of heat and agitation showed in her cheeks which were a bright hot pink and in her eyes which seemed larger and were slightly shadowed.

She rolled down her stockings and slipped them off her feet. The skin of her legs was white and she thought enviously of Juanita's tan, set off to such advantage by the colour-splashed sun-dress. She was glad Juanita was young

39

and friendly. The friendliness and sympathy had dispelled to a certain extent the dismay and disappointment she had felt when she had learned that her escort from the airport was Roger Gallant.

Whatever had led her to talk to him about Transmarine's plans to buy the Gallant estate, and to criticise so freely a person she had never met who had turned out to be himself? She should have remembered that a secretary should not chatter away to all and sundry about her boss's business.

But Roger Gallant had been so friendly and kind that it had been hard not to talk to him.

That's no excuse, Miranda! She could almost hear Aunt Clara cautioning her about the inadvisability of talking to complete strangers. Well, she had disobeyed that advice and had been deceived.

When she considered the matter more carefully she could see that Roger had probably been angry because he had been deceived too by Mr Ingram, and she could not condone her boss's tactics to entice the elusive composer to come on the cruise to discuss the future of the Gallant estate. Only a short time ago she had been defending Mr Ingram, saying he would never do anything underhand. How foolish she must have seemed to Roger, who had known by then just how underhand Mr Ingram could be.

A knock on the door brought her to her feet. She opened it. A young man about her own age stood there. He was big and muscular and was dressed in shorts and a T-shirt. His hair was longish and dark brown, inclined to curl, and his eyes were a sleepy faded blue. At his feet were her two cases. He grinned and held put a large hand to her.

'I'm Chuck Gallant,' he said. 'Nita asked me to bring your cases. Glad to meet you.'

Miranda shook his hand and smiled back.

'Thank you. Could you please put them over there.'

He carried them easily to the space beside the chest of drawers, then turned to look at her again.

'I hope you're going to dinner with us tonight,' he said.

'I'm glad to see you're not middle-aged or married like everyone else on this tub. I was beginning to get the idea I'd made one big mistake by coming, but now that you've come and Roger has turned up things look more interesting. Rog always livens things up a bit even if it's only by tormenting my father. He's a great guy, but mischievous, if you get me. Can you swim?'

'A little.'

'That's great. Perhaps we'll be able to go snorkelling or even diving. There's plenty of equipment on the yacht and a small sailing boat.' He moved towards the door and raised a big hand in casual farewell. 'See you,' he murmured, and slid out of the door.

Alone once more, Miranda opened one of her cases and took out her toilet things and a nightdress. A shower, a sleep between cool sheets in an air-conditioned room, that was all she desired, for the present.

Miranda slept soundly, but towards the end of her sleep she dreamed that she was swimming in warm greenish water which caressed her skin like silk. After a while she realised she was under water and weaving in and out of great masses of coral as if she were a fish. She had a desperate desire to find her way out of the maze of coral and float upwards to the surface, but something was holding her foot. The more she struggled the tighter the unseen manacle became. She looked back and saw reddish-brown seaweed floating behind and above her. As she watched, it turned into hair. Someone was floating beside her wearing a snorkelling mask so that she couldn't see his eyes or face. A voice drawled,

'You're caught now. There's no escape. You've caught the Gallant's Fancy, Miranda, the Gallant's Fancy, Miranda, Miranda ...'

A voice was repeating her name over and over again. She opened her eyes and saw someone bending over her. Grey hair set in severe crisp waves. Diamonds glinting in ears and round a full plump neck. Heavy, recently-tanned features, a bright smile. Zelda Ingram.

'Miranda! Time to wake up. We're all going to have dinner ashore and Doug would like to see you in his office before we set off.'

Miranda struggled to a sitting position. One of her feet was tangled in a sheet, which must have given her the impression in the dream that there had been a manacle round her ankle. She blinked in the light shed from the big table lamp which stood on the chest of drawers. Her glance went to the portholes. Blue and white curtains had been pulled across them. It must be dark outside already.

'What time is it?' she asked.

'Seven-thirty. I hope you feel better after your little nap. So wise of you to have a sleep after that long journey. I hope you've brought something suitable to wear for dining out. Anything long?'

Zelda was wearing a smooth black dress with long sleeves and a scooped out neckline which made her appear slimmer than she was.

'A long skirt and a frilly blouse,' said Miranda.

'Ideal. Now dress quickly and go along to Doug's office. Take the tapes and correspondence with you. He won't keep you for long—it's just to put you in the picture with regard to the people he has invited. We're going to have such a lovely time. Imagine, flamenco dancers, and we're not even in Spain!'

When Mrs Ingram had gone Miranda dressed in the long skirt of deep blue and the sheer white frilly blouse which she had bought for such an occasion as dining out. She brushed her hair until it was shining and applied a little make-up. Then, collecting the tapes and files of letters she had brought, she made her way to the cabin which Doug Ingram had set aside as his office for the period of the cruise.

Tall and handsome, he looked even more handsome in a white tuxedo, white shirt and dark bow tie and dark trousers. Formal clothes set off his spare upright figure and white-winged dark hair. The day in the sun had given his face a distinguished tan which emphasised the hard uncompromising grey of his eyes and made him seem younger than his fifty-odd years.

'I'm glad to see you, Miranda,' he greeted her coolly. 'Put the tapes over there. I regret I wasn't here when you arrived with Roger Gallant. I thought he was coming on a later flight from New York. I wanted to be here to explain why so many of his relatives were on board and tell him the reason for the cruise myself. However, I gather from the brief conversation I had with him before going to change for dinner that you took care of that explanation for me.'

There was a dreadful little silence while those hard grey eyes bored into hers. Miranda licked her lips and said softly:

'He was rather angry.'

'Naturally. However, he seems to have taken it better from a pretty girl like you than perhaps he would have done from me. He was very much at home up in the bar and seemed extremely pleased to see Mrs Dawn Gallant. So all is well. But, and it's a big but, Miranda, do be careful about what you say to these Gallants. They need to be handled very diplomatically.'

'Yes, Mr Ingram. I'm sorry. You see...' Miranda stopped speaking when he held up a hand and smiled at her.

'No apologies and no explanations this time, Miranda. I'm quite aware you were ignorant of the identity of your escort. It's just possible that we can turn your little mistake to our advantage.'

'In what way?' asked Miranda uneasily.

'From the brief conversation I had with him I gather that you've caught Roger Gallant's fancy and I'd like you to use his interest in you, encourage it, if you will, in order to further our cause which is to persuade him to sell his share of the Gallant estate, as you know.' Mr Ingram paused and frowned reflectively, then continued blandly, 'He isn't an easy man to approach, as I discovered in New York. If I'd

43

laid my cards on the table then I'm sure he wouldn't have come on this cruise. However, it's possible he'll listen to a woman's point of view, and now that he's here with the rest of the family, all of whom are keen not only to have Fortuga put on the map as a holiday resort but also to make a little money too, I hope he'll come down from his cloud-cuckoo land and accept our offer for the whole of the estate.'

Although inwardly astounded at the thought of deliberately having to set out and encourage any man's interest in her with a view to persuading him to do something he didn't wish to do, Miranda answered dutifully:

'Yes, Mr Ingram. It would help a little if I knew more about the property. I'm not quite clear as to who owns what.'

'I agree,' said Mr Ingram. 'It would be better if you knew exactly, wouldn't it. Then there'll be less chance of you making any more faux pas.'

Although his smile was amiable Miranda couldn't help flinching and she felt the blood rise in her cheeks.

'According to Thomas Gallant, who's a rogue if ever there was one,' continued Mr Ingram, 'Fortuga has quite an interesting and romantic history. It was first settled by a Spaniard whose family name was Fortuga. Then a pirate from Devon, England, called Richard Gallant came across it. It caught his fancy, as did the beautiful daughter of the Spaniard. He raided the island, slew the Spaniard, married the daughter and re-named the island Gallant's Fancy.'

Miranda started, recalling her recent dream, and he gave her a curious glance.

'Something wrong?' he asked.

'No. It's rather a strange name, that's all,' she mumbled defensively.

'But descriptive,' remarked Mr Ingram drily. 'Well, to cut the story short, in later years the island reverted to the original Spanish name and Gallant's Fancy was given to that part of the land owned by the elder son of the pirate, while that of Gallant's Folly was given to the land owned by the younger son. Now, according to an old entail, which is still in force, neither part can be sold without the other. As you might guess, Mr Thomas Gallant is the owner of Gallant's Folly and Mr Roger Gallant is the owner of the Fancy. The house of the latter is, by the way, built on an excellent site and was occupied until quite recently. It would make the perfect nucleus for a new hotel.'

'I think it's still occupied, Mr Ingram,' said Miranda quietly.

'Oh? What's led you to think that?' he asked, giving her a sharp appraising glance.

'Something Mr Roger Gallant said to his cousin the Señora. He mentioned a person called Marnie who he thinks should be here to join in the discussions about the property.'

'Aha! I can see, Miranda, that you have a good ear and are a picker up of trifles which could be of use to us. See if you can find out more about Marnie, please. And now we mustn't keep the others waiting any longer. Just bear in mind what I've told you and do what you can.'

'Yes, Mr Ingram, I'll do my best.'

'I'm sure you will. That's why I asked for you to be sent out here.'

Night had spread a black velvet cloak across the sky and it was sprinkled with sparkling diamonds. In the harbour the big cruise ships scintillated with lights which were reflected in the dark water, like stars in the sea. The air was warm and fragrant with the scent of numerous flowering bushes.

It seemed to Miranda that the atmosphere was charged with magic and she felt her spirits lift in excited anticipation as she walked through the old town of San Juan to the restaurant where they were to have dinner.

The street was narrow and lined with high Spanish walls. Through arched doorways open to the night she caught glimpses of dimly-lit interiors in which bottles gleamed

45

ruby and amber from shelves and oblique light burnished the moustachioed swarthy faces of men leaning on bars, and the soft hum of conversation was accompanied by the passionate throb of a guitar.

She crossed a street of brightly lit shops. It was thronged with big cars, all moving at a snail's pace in the narrow confines. Each car was filled to capacity with Puerto Ricans determined to enjoy their night out. On her left a square of elegant floodlit buildings opened up. Graceful trees cast a delicate tracery of shadow on bleached stone and in the centre a young man stood on a wooden platform and harangued passionately a group of noisy youths.

The restaurant which Doug Ingram had chosen was cosy and welcoming. The décor was entirely Spanish; tan walls and dark woodwork, a low-beamed ceiling, wrought iron railings. The proprietor, a fine figure in tight-fitting grey suit piped with black velvet, a lacy shirt and cravat and a red cummerbund, greeted them personally and conducted them to their tables.

To her relief Miranda was seated at the same table as Juanita, Ramon and Chuck. At the other table sat the Ingrams, Thomas Gallant and his wife Dawn, who was all silver and mother-of-pearl, seeming to glow with her own ethereal light in that dim room. Beside Dawn sat Roger, but a different Roger from the friendly young man in blue jeans who had escorted Miranda from the airport that afternoon. Now he appeared suave and sophisticated, elegantly dressed in a lightweight cream suit which he wore with a black shirt and a brightly hued tie. To Miranda he was as unapproachable as any other celebrity would be and she felt an inner cringing from the task which Mr Ingram had set her. How could she, a simple, small town girl, hope to encourage the interest of anyone like Roger Gallant, who had only to enter a room or sit at a table for women to turn and glance at him with interest lighting their eyes?

Ramon, Juanita's husband, was a happy-go-lucky young man, small and slim with a head of thick wavy black hair,

46

black eyes and a flashing white smile beneath a droopy black moustache. He loved parties, he told Miranda, and was determined to enjoy this one.

'Puerto Rico is the gourmet centre of the Caribbean islands,' he announced boastfully. 'Our breadbasket is international, thanks to the Spanish ships which used to sail here. Not one of them was allowed to come here without bringing plants from other parts of the Spanish Empire. As a result we now grow oranges from Spain, bananas from Africa, pineapples from the South Sea islands, sugar-cane from India.'

Persuaded by him, Miranda ate juicy fresh nuggets of lobster swimming in a delicious baffling sauce which he told her was made from tomatoes and egg-plants. Her dessert was a fluffy masterpiece made from egg yolks and liqueur. The wine was light and sparkling and the conversation matched it. All the time they were eating guitars strummed not only the haunting music of old Spain but also lively familiar Latin-American rhythms.

When the leisurely meal was over they strolled through the narrow streets to a night club. Tucked away in the cavernous recesses of an old building, it looked from the outside like one of the little bars Miranda had noticed on the way to the restaurant. But at the back of the little bar they passed through a red velvet curtain into an inner room. There white walls, a series of arches leading from one area to another and more fringed red curtains emphasised the Iberian atmosphere. Light was from the single candles on each table and from the spotlight trained on the dancer who moved stiffly, with a rhythmical tapping of heels, across a stage.

For a while Miranda watched the dancer. He was dressed in tight-fitting white dungaree-style pants over a full-sleeved black shirt and had a black sombrero tilted over his narrow dark face. His dancing had a hypnotic effect and it was some time before she could look away. Then her glance strayed, searching for Roger, wondering how he felt about

47

being back in the place where he had written the music for the song which had brought success both to himself and his friend Kit Williams.

He was sitting at another table, leaning back indolently in his chair, and he wasn't watching the dancer. He was staring at herself. The upward flare of the candlelight emphasised his finely-chiselled face and it seemed to Miranda that twin flames danced in his eyes, reflections of the flame of the candle.

She could not hold back the sudden sweep of colour to her cheeks as she encountered his enigmatic gaze. Around her the atmosphere of the cave-like room seemed sultry in spite of air-conditioning. The steady strumming of guitars, the thudding of the dancer's feet stirred the blood and increased the pulse rate. She was acutely aware of everything; of the rich fragrance of cigar smoke mingling with the exotic perfumes worn by some of the women; of the sensual sheen of white or burnished-brown bare skin contrasted against sombre or brilliantly coloured stuffs of suits or dresses; of hidden primitive desires revealing themselves in the glint of an eye or the tensing of a muscle; above all she was aware of the attractive curve of a man's mouth as he smiled at her.

Movement broke the spell which had bound her briefly. A man had approached Roger. Her heart beating wildly, she looked at the dancer again. There was safety in watching the tapping heels.

What had happened to her? Who was this creature whose heart was throbbing and whose cheeks were glowing just because a man who was virtually a stranger had looked at her and had smiled at her in a subtly inviting way?

It must be the place, the sound of guitars and the glow of candlelight, the stamping of feet in regular rhythm and the sense of latent passion. All heady stuff for a young woman like herself who had been brought up in the cool, astringent atmosphere of a home ruled over by a spinster aunt.

She had a longing for the coolness of Aunt Clara's house,

for the uncomplicated way of life there. Her throat felt parched and she seized the drink which had been placed before her. It was long and cool and when she tasted it fruity bubbles burst against her palate and the ice bobbing near the surface soothed her hot mouth.

The dancing came to an abrupt end. Tumultuous applause broke out. The dancer took his bow many times. Miranda sipped some more of her delicious fruit concoction and glanced once more, surreptitiously this time in case she encountered another enigmatic glance from Roger, at the next table.

Shock tingled through her. His chair was empty. So was the one next to it where Dawn Gallant had been sitting. They had gone, while the applause was at its loudest and no one had noticed them going.

In fact Thomas Gallant did not notice that his wife was missing until the time came for them all to leave the night-club and find their way along the narrow streets, where shadowy figures lingered on the high balconies and dim stairways led up from arched open doorways.

'Wow! Pop's pretty mad,' chortled Chuck. 'Listen to him!' From behind came the sound of Thomas Gallant's full-throated roar as in uninhibited language he called his cousin names for stealing his wife.

'Let's get away from him,' urged Juanita, hurrying down the street and pulling Miranda with her. 'Oh, how ashamed he makes me feel when he behaves like that in public! Roger is just as bad in his own way. He knew Dawn would go with him if he asked her, and he asked her to annoy Father. You must think we're a dreadful family, Miranda. I can assure you we're not all like that. Chuck, Marnie and I are quite normal. It's just those two who behave like pirates, stealing from one another all the time. Throwbacks, both of them.'

Down the street they hurried, the heels of their high-heeled sandals clicking on the broken uneven sidewalk.

'Stealing?' Ramon had caught up with them and was

FANCY

placing an arm around the waist of his tempestuous wife to slow her down. 'Who has been stealing?'

'I was talking of my father and Roger. They're like those two early Gallants, the sons of the pirate who's supposed to have settled Fortuga.'

'And what have they been stealing from each other this time?' asked Chuck, who had come up on the other side of Miranda. Much to her surprise he slipped his arm round her waist in a curiously possessive fashion.

'This time it's Dawn,' said Juanita fiercely. 'Once it was Josephine.'

'Forgive me, but I'm lost,' laughed Ramon. 'Who is Josephine?'

'She used to work for Father, at the house on Fortuga. Marnie said . . .' Juanita broke off abruptly.

'Go on, what did Marnie say?' urged Chuck curiously.

'Oh, nothing. It doesn't matter. She could have been mistaken,' muttered Juanita. Then with a change of tone she added, 'Look, Miranda, we're coming to the gate of the Cristo Chapel. Isn't it beautiful?'

The end of the street was closed to motor vehicles by a chain slung between two old stone posts across the cobbled street. Beyond that was a sturdily built square tower with a wide open arched entrance. The interior of the tower was painted white and at the rear of it was another arch in which there was an intricately-carvèd wrought iron gate. On top of the tower was an ornate piece of stonework from which a bell was hung. The whole building was floodlit from lights hung above the roadway and by old-fashioned lanterns which jutted out from the buildings on either side. In the blaze of light the golden stone of the ancient gate glowed with almost unearthly glamour, like the gate to paradise might glow, thought Miranda fancifully.

Turning aside from the gate, they plunged down another dark street which wound down to the harbour.

'Who is Marnie?' Miranda asked Chuck, wondering what Joe would say if he could see her now, tripping down a

50

street in San Juan at one o'clock in the morning with a young man's arm around her waist.

'She's Roger's sister, and if we should ever get to Fortuga on this cruise you'll meet her, because she lives in the house known as Gallant's Fancy. She's a bit of a recluse because she's blind,' replied Chuck.

They reached the bottom of the hill crossed the wide street and found the wharf where the *Sea Quest* was tied up. The big cruise ship was leaving, going astern with much thrashing of water and throbbing of engines. From its decks passengers waved farewell to San Juan as they set off on their vacation amongst the islands.

'We're leaving as soon as it's light,' said Chuck, as he followed Miranda up the gangway and on to the yacht. 'I heard Doug Ingram say he hoped to be in St Thomas by lunch time tomorrow. Let's hope we have a smooth passage.'

From the way they were settling into loungers on the side-deck of *Sea Quest* it looked as if he and the Delgados were prepared to wait up until first light, thought Miranda as fatigue caught her unexpectedly behind the knees and at the back of the eyes. The energy and capacity for pleasure had gone. He called to her and so, making her excuses, she said good-night.

Immediately Chuck was on his feet to escort her to the door of her cabin. Outside the door he grinned down at her cheekily.

'I guess you're not up to it yet, Miranda,' he remarked. 'It'll take a day or two for you to adjust to the change in time.'

Just at that moment from further along the passage they heard the boom of Thomas Gallant's voice. He had apparently gone straight to his cabin and had found his wife there already.

'Well, how the hell was I to know where you'd gone? I turned round to say something to you and you were missing, so naturally I thought you'd gone off somewhere to-

51

gether for the night. All right, so I was wrong...'

A door crashed angrily closed and the voice became a muffled roar.

This time Chuck's grin was a trifle shamefaced.

'He isn't always like that,' he explained. 'He feels a little insecure where Dawn is concerned. She's much younger than he is and very attractive, and Roger is, or can be when he wants to be, a gallant in more senses than one, and if you're not sure of the meanings of the word I suggest you look them up in a dictionary before you too succumb to that fatal charm. G'night, Miranda. With a bit of luck we should be able to swim tomorrow.'

Miranda slept all night without a dream. She awoke to the dull throb of two heavy diesel engines and lay watching the quivering reflection of light on the white ceiling of the cabin, trying to remember where she was and what had happened.

All the previous day's happenings came rushing back, jumbling in her mind in a kaleidoscope of faces and scenes. She sprang out of bed and immediately lost her balance. The yacht was rolling, a slight insidious motion, not enough to upset the stomach but enough to make one aware that the yacht was at sea.

Through the porthole she saw an expanse of deep blue sea, ruffled by wind and gilded by sunlight. Over it arched the sky, a slightly paler blue which was cloudless.

Excitement made her move quickly. She must not miss a moment of this adventure. Dressing swiftly, she noticed that it was seven o'clock. Mr Ingram had said he would not require her this morning, so for several hours she was free to do as she wished. She would go to the highest deck she could find and see what she could see.

Although the smell of breakfast cooking lingered in the air there was no one about on the main deck. Finding a doorway, Miranda went through it on to a side-deck. The morning breeze caught at the full skirt of her cotton shirt-waister and blew it upwards so that she wished she had had

52

the sense to wear trousers or shorts. Not wishing to waste any time, she held it down to her sides and went up a flight of steps on to the sun-deck.

Going as far forward as she could, she leaned on the rails. In the blue distance islands loomed, but the glare of sunlight on the sea was already too bright for her to look for long. She had forgotten to bring her sun-glasses so she shaded her eyes with both hands. At once her skirt, unrestrained by her hands, blew up again.

'You seem to be having problems this morning,' said a voice with an undercurrent of laughter lilting through it, and she turned to find Roger leaning on the rail beside her. As she might have guessed, he was dressed ideally for the weather and situation in white well-fitting pants belted at the waist, a navy-blue cotton shirt open at the neck, and rope-soled espadrilles on his bare feet. His smoothly brushed hair glinted with coppery light and his eyes were hidden by the inevitable baffling sun-glasses.

'I didn't realise it would be so breezy,' she replied.

'Or so bright, early in the morning,' he put in. 'You should wear a hat, Miranda.'

'Oh, I didn't think,' she began, a little flustered by his personal interest. 'I haven't brought one.'

'Then I shall buy one for you in St Thomas,' he answered gaily, with a glimmer of a smile. 'We mustn't let that enviable English complexion be ruined by our too strong sun. Have you forgiven me for yesterday's little deception yet?'

'Oh, yes,' said Miranda, smiling back spontaneously. She was always ready to forgive anyone, and he seemed so sincere in the early morning light that she forgot Mr Ingram's instructions and Chuck's warning and responded just as sincerely. 'And thank you for staying and explaining to Mr Ingram. You see, if you'd left before he'd come back from the beach I might have lost my job.'

'I wouldn't like to have been the cause of that,' he replied gravely.

'I'm afraid Mr Ingram deceived you. I'm sorry about that,' she offered hesitantly, and he turned his head sharply to look at her. Then his smile made two attractive creases in his lean cheeks and the wind lifted the chestnut-brown hair from his forehead as he leaned back against the rail so that he could face her.

'That's nice of you, Miranda. Am I to believe from that remark that his tactics to get me on board this yacht and meet my cousins didn't receive your approval?'

'Naturally I wasn't consulted,' she answered with a quiet dignity which made his smile deepen, 'but when I learned that he had deceived you I was a little upset. I'm afraid I'm not very knowledgeable about big business. This is the first time I've acted as a full-time secretary. I have a lot to learn.'

'Then let me give you a tip. All's fair in love and war, and today you might as well regard business as done by companies such as yours as war. It's a struggle for power.' He paused, then added with a faintly impish grin, 'Do you know about love? Or do I have to explain that to you too?'

'A little,' replied Miranda primly. 'I don't agree with you that it's like war.'

'The way we Gallants love it is,' he murmured, and immediately she was reminded of the previous evening when he had left the night-club and had taken his cousin's wife with him. 'You don't look as if you're in love or have ever been in love, Miranda,' was his next amazingly frank comment.

'Well, I am,' she retorted. 'And when I return to England I'm going to be married.'

'To a young man you've known for years, sound of character, who'll keep you safe and secure for the rest of your days,' he said rather drily. 'He's to be congratulated on having been so astute as to have chosen someone like you.'

He lunged away from the rail and turned again to look at the sea. Acutely aware of a sudden change in his mood, Miranda flicked an uneasy glance at his face. There was a touch of bitterness to the curve of his mouth now. He had withdrawn and his thoughts were moving down paths of which she had no knowledge and which gave him no pleasure.

'Is the sea always as blue as this?' she asked a little nervously, in an attempt to break through the barrier which he had thrown up.

'Nearly always,' he answered rather vaguely, and silence followed, a silence emphasized by the throb of the engines and the rushing sound of water beneath the hull of the yacht. They were approaching an island closely now. It was no longer blue, but a series of curving hills covered with thick green vegetation.

'Is that St Thomas?' asked Miranda, still nervous.

Her companion made an obvious effort to throw off his more sombre mood and turned to look at her again.

'It is—the old haunt of English buccaneers such as Blackbeard and Sir Henry Morgan. In fact one of the hills used to be called Blackbeard's Hill because he had a watchtower built on it. Sir Francis Drake also came this way, and there's a story that it was he who gave the Virgin Islands their name, calling them after Elizabeth the First, who was the Virgin Queen. Another story says that Columbus, who discovered them, gave them their name. Later the Danes took over some of the islands and you'll find many Danish names as well as Spanish and English and French ones. Have you had breakfast yet?'

'No.'

'Come and have it with me, then, and I shall tell you all about the wicked English pirates and you can tell me,' he paused, then added wickedly, 'all about Transmarine's plans for Fortuga.'

In the days that followed, even in years long afterwards, Miranda never forgot that first morning in the Caribbean when she took breakfast with Roger aboard the *Sea Quest* as the yacht thrust forward through the sparkling blue water.

They sat at a small table under an awning outside the main saloon and were waited on by a young steward called Billy, whose white shirt was dazzling against his brown skin and whose grin was as white as the shirt. While they ate she and Roger talked not about the pirates or Transmarine, but about themselves. He learned all about Aunt Clara and Dottie and just a little about Joe, and she learned all about his grandmother Fiona MacGregor who had gone from the Highlands of Scotland to teach music and other ladylike pursuits to a family of girls in Trinidad, had met a certain Rupert Gallant from Fortuga and had married him. It was Fiona who had recognised the musical talent of her youngest grandson and had given him a piano, on which, for as long as he could remember, he had picked out tunes of his own invention.

By the time they had finished eating the yacht had entered a wide almost land-locked bay and Miranda had her first sight of Charlotte Amalie, the chief town of the island of St Thomas, named after a Danish queen.

Sea Quest was tied up by the stern at the waterfront which ran along the front of the town on the northern side of the harbour. There were other private motor yachts similar to *Sea Quest* already there, and the convenience of tying up there was soon apparent to Miranda when she stepped down the gangway with Roger and within a few minutes was strolling up a pleasant passageway between two buildings, towards the main shopping street. The passage was shaded by palm trees and other tropical plants and on either side were the entrances to small shops which offered goods varying from paintings by local artists to craftwork imported from other countries.

It was a town which bustled and rushed like any other harbour town and it was stocked with merchandise from every country in the world. Its history was depicted in its architecture. The Danish-style houses had Spanish patios and there was a hint of French colonial style here and there. New buildings were American in style.

True to his promise Roger took Miranda to a big shop bearing a Danish name where fine quality goods were set out in tempting array in an old concrete warehouse. He chose and paid for the hat she would wear. It was a white open straw with a wide brim. When she asked him how much it had cost so that she could pay for it, he did not seem to hear but paid for it himself. Then he guided her from the shop down another fascinating palm-shaded passage to sit outside a café at a round table and to drink ice-cold beer.

They visited other shops and Miranda bought a halter-necked sun-dress and another bikini. Then they wandered along the main street, which was thronged with tourists, all looking for duty-free bargains to take back home.

At a corner Miranda paused to admire a collection of huge conch shells which a street vendor had on show. The vendor was a young woman whose long blonde hair contrasted strikingly with her deeply tanned face. In answer to Miranda's questions she explained that she and her brother dived for the beautiful shells. They ate the meat, then cleaned and sterilised the shells for sale.

To Miranda's surprise Roger bought a shell and then presented it to her.

Her eyes on the beautiful cream and pink shell which he held between his hands, she said rather shyly:

'You mustn't give me presents. Please let me pay you for this and the hat.'

'Now *I* am offended,' he replied. 'Why shouldn't I give you things which you like? They're not bribes, you know, I don't want anything in return.'

They stood on the edge of the teeming sidewalk as they faced each other, tension springing between them. In spite of the bright sunlight, the brilliant colours, the jostling crowds of tourists Miranda was back in the dark cave of the night-club in San Juan, seeing him smile at her with subtle invitation. He wasn't smiling now. His mouth was stern, but she wished she could see his eyes!

'That wasn't a very nice thing to say,' she said quietly, her voice quivering a little, her grey eyes beneath the shadow of the brim of her white hat wide and hurt.

'No, it wasn't, but that's how you see my gifts, isn't it? I'd forgotten that English girls aren't accustomed to receiving gifts from men.' He showed sudden uncertainty by biting his lower lip with white teeth. The uncertainty didn't last long, for he smiled almost tenderly at her. 'Please, Miranda, will you accept this shell from me, because it's given me such pleasure to be with you this morning and to watch your face as you've looked, admired and exclaimed. I've been seeing this town through your eyes and it's become a place of charm and beauty instead of the commercial congested centre I know it to be.'

He held the shell out to her again. It glowed with reflected light, a thing of natural beauty which would be a joy for ever. Miranda knew that whenever she looked at it in the future she would remember that morning spent with Roger in the town of Charlotte Amalie.

'Thank you,' she said, and the pink which glowed in her cheeks vied with the pink of the shell. 'You're very kind.'

'No, I'm not kind, and don't you forget it,' he said roughly. 'I think we'd better return to the yacht. I believe an outing is planned for this afternoon to the new hotel which Transmarine is building on the other side of the island. We're to motor round there in the yacht and anchor in the bay. We'll go ashore and take our time to admire the quality of the construction, the superiority of the architecture and the exceptional facilities offered in the complete holiday resort which Transmarine offers all over the world.'

The sarcasm in his voice hurt her. He was attacking all that she believed to be true about the company she worked for. For some reason he disliked big organisations. Feeling as he did he could have left yesterday afternoon when he had discovered the real reason for the cruise, but he had stayed. Why? She was too modest to think that he had stayed to help her out of a difficult situation. Had he stayed because he had found his cousin's wife was on board and he had wished to revive a past affair with her? Or had he some other deeper reason?

By the time they reached the yacht it was ready to leave the waterfront. Roger and Miranda went up to the bar on the sun-deck where they found Dawn and Chuck already helping themselves to pre-luncheon drinks.

'Where did you get to?' asked Chuck, coming across to Miranda and looking down at her possessively, then giving Roger a fierce under-browed glance.

'You should get up earlier,' mocked Roger. 'Then *you* could take her shopping.'

He moved past them towards the bar where Dawn was perched on a stool, sipping a drink from a tall frosted glass. She was wearing a long sleeveless beach gown. It was made from white lace and through the openwork her smooth bronzed skin gleamed provocatively.

'What would you like to drink, Miranda?' Roger asked, and he went behind the bar.

'Something fruity and thirst-quenching, please,' she replied, sitting down in one of the comfortable padded chairs. She was glad to be back in the air-conditioned yacht because the heat of the day had begun to make her feel quite tired.

'Try one of these,' drawled Dawn. 'A rum base and pineapple and banana juice.'

'That's no way to drink good rum, which this is,' scoffed Roger as he placed a bottle of amber liquid on the top of the bar. 'And you as the wife of a Gallant should know by now that the only way to drink good rum is in the same way you should drink good whisky, with only water added. Where's Tom? Still sleeping off last night?'

He was different, superficial and shallow, his voice a studied taunt, his eyes narrowed and bright, his mouth sardonic. Miranda could only stare at him, bemused, and wonder what had happened to her attentive gallant of the morning.

59

'Was he mad last night!' sighed Dawn. 'I should never have gone with you, Roger.'

'Regretting it already?' he countered, busy with bottles of fruit juice and a shaker.

'No, but I was surprised he objected to me going with you. He doesn't usually mind when I go off with someone else.'

'Where did you go anyway?' asked Chuck.

'That would be telling, honey-child,' murmured Dawn provocatively, sending a stream of cigarette smoke in his direction.

'We went to another dive in old San Juan, to escape the limelight which Luiz Benitz was determined to turn on me,' remarked Roger drily. 'Here you are, Miranda. All fruit juice and ice, concocted especially to quench that thirst.'

He brought the drink over to her, smiled briefly when she thanked him and went to lean against the bar close to Dawn.

'Roger, I must talk to you,' said Dawn urgently. 'Alone.'

'Not before lunch,' he drawled lazily, and took a sip of his rum and water. 'And never, if it's about Gallant's Fancy.'

'Why won't you agree to sell it?' Dawn complained.

'Because it's Marnie's home even if by law and inheritance I'm the owner.'

'She could live somewhere else,' persisted Dawn, ignoring his desire not to discuss the disposal of the estate. 'She could live anywhere, it wouldn't matter. She can't see, so what difference does it make where she lives?'

Miranda flinched at the careless callousness of Dawn's speech and looked at Roger to see his reaction. Apart from a faint frown between his finely marked eyebrows he showed no emotion.

'It matters a great deal,' he replied coolly. 'Marnie knows the Fancy and loves it. The people of the island know and love her. It makes a great difference when you're blind if you know you're surrounded by familiar objects and

60

familiar people. If she lived anywhere else she would wither away and die.' The cool voice faltered slightly and he added in a lower tone, 'Then I'd have that on my conscience as well as her blindness.'

'But Tom needs the money, and you know he can't sell the Folly without the Fancy,' cried Dawn petulantly.

'That's Tom's tough luck. Has it never occurred to him that there are others he should consult before any sale of property is made to Transmarine? How does he know what the people of Fortuga want? He's never given them a thought in the whole of his lazy selfish life.' Now Roger's voice was more than cool. It was ice-cold, crisp and curt. Even a stranger coming into the room would know that he had no liking for his cousin. 'Is he sure they want to be developed in the same way as other islands? Does he think that Aubrey Vincent and Sam Williams have no say in the matter?'

'Surely anything would be better for them than rotting amongst the banana bush and the sugar cane,' retorted Dawn tartly. 'Oh, you islanders are all the same, sentimental and romantic, living in the past. But I find it hard to believe that you're any less selfish than Tom. Since when have you done anything for the island?'

'I've done very little, I admit, but I won't let Transmarine take it over,' he replied quietly.

'You don't want to sell just to spite Tom,' Dawn flung at him suddenly raging. 'It's O.K. for you. You've done nothing but rake in royalties ever since you wrote the music for that song. Kit Williams hasn't done badly either, so I don't suppose the Williams tribe suffer much. As for Aubrey Vincent, everyone knows he's sitting pretty with Marnie as his boss.'

'It's a pity,' said Roger in a voice which was as smooth as silk, although his eyes held a dangerous glitter, 'that Tom has never been able to choose a wife to suit his pocket. Why should I sell Marnie's home just to put mink on your back, Dawn? Tell me that.'

61

FANCY

Dawn was on her feet in a second. She hurled the remains of her drink at Roger who, anticipating her action, sidestepped so that the rum and fruit juice spattered the floor harmlessly.

'I hate you, Roger Gallant, hate you! Do you hear?' she yelled.

'I hear, and so can everyone else on the yacht,' he replied with a taunting grin. 'I warned you, didn't I, that I didn't want to discuss the matter with you. Why don't you forget it while we're on this cruise, then you and I can have some fun?' He glanced at Miranda and his grin widened. 'You've shocked Miranda by that little exhibition. She's not used to such violent uninhibited behaviour.'

With a smothered imprecation Dawn swept out of the room and Roger turned his attention to Chuck.

'Why is Tom in a bad way financially?' he asked.

'Well—er—you hit the nail on the head when you mentioned mink,' said Chuck, looking rather uncomfortable. 'Dawn has run up some fantastic bills and he still pays alimony to my mother.'

'He's always been greedy, and now he's paying for it,' remarked Roger coldly. 'What about you? Have you finished law school yet?'

'No. I've had to take a year off because Pop couldn't come up with the fees,' muttered Chuck sulkily. 'Oh, you needn't look like that. I've been working, but I took time off to come on this jaunt because as Tom's heir I'm interested in what happens to the property. Is there any way of getting round that old entail?'

'I don't know. You're the lawyer. Why don't you find out?'

'If only we could sell the Folly without touching the Fancy,' suggested Chuck hopefully.

'You seem to have forgotten one important point. Ingram has now decided that without the Fancy the Folly is no good to him. You see, he's discovered that the Folly's house

62

is built on a swamp and is falling down,' replied Roger blandly.

'You told him,' accused Chuck.

'Of course I did.' He looked at Miranda and added rather sourly, 'Well, Miranda, there's plenty for you to report back to your boss, isn't there?'

She caught her breath in sudden pain. The taunt was a barb which found a sensitive spot.

'Do you think I would report everything to him?' she protested, reproach in her clear candid eyes. She had finished her drink and was sitting with the conch shell between her hands, a quiet dark-haired girl whose cheeks seemed to reflect the pink of the shell.

Some of the hardness went from his face and eyes as his gaze held hers for a strangely intimate moment.

'No, I don't think you would willingly,' he conceded, 'but when he asks you what you and I have been talking about all morning you'll have to tell him something, won't you?'

He was right, of course. She could hardly tell Mr Ingram that her conversation with Roger that morning had ranged over various topics from Aunt Clara to the songs sung to Roger when he was a child by his Caribbean nannie, the lilting melodies of which had found their way into his own music.

No, she couldn't tell Mr Ingram about her morning with Roger. That was a secret to be hugged to herself for the rest of her life. In the future she would remember, at quiet moments alone in her suburban home in England, the dangerous delight she had experienced while lingering in the palm-shaded passages of Charlotte Amalie with a young man who had given her a conch shell, and she would wonder whether it had really happened.

So after lunch, when she had finished typing some letters for Mr Ingram she told him, in answer to his questions, the little she had learned about blind Marnie and Roger's reason for not wishing to sell Gallant's Fancy. He listened intently and then gave her a shrewd glance and said:

'I see. Well, I think we can deal with that little problem. I don't think a blind woman will stand in our way for long. Thank you, Miranda, for the information.'

His attitude struck a chill into her. Looking at him closely she could see now that his eyes were quite cold and empty of feeling. He did not care about other people, only about business and his own ambition to pull off another big deal.

'This afternoon I'd like you to come with us on a tour of the hotel site. You can take notes. Tomorrow we'll leave St Thomas and visit another of the Virgin Islands,' he announced. 'I've decided to spend a week amongst them in order to build up an atmosphere of mutual trust and confidence. It will be time well spent. Be as pleasant as you can to Roger, but at the same time put the mind of Chuck at rest. He has the impatience of the young. He needs the money for college and is likely to encourage his father to sell to another bidder if we dally too long. I think there's a possibility of enlisting Mrs Gallant's assistance in the gentle art of persuasion. She and Roger were once friendly, and I think it's time that their friendship was revived.'

CHAPTER THREE

THE afternoon sun was hot, shining down out of a cloudless sky, striking diamond-bright sparks of light from the chromium-plated fittings of the big sleek motor yacht *Sea Quest*, which was tied up at the small dock on an island in the Virgin group which, once deserted, was now in the process of being developed by Transmarine Holdings.

Since leaving St Thomas the party aboard the yacht had spent seven lazy days loitering about the small bays and inlets of the Virgin Islands, dawdling along that most beautiful of waterways, Sir Francis Drake's Channel. The perfect weather, sunshine and a steady trade wind blowing, plus the easy-going way of life on board ship, had slowly built up that atmosphere of trust and confidence which Mr Ingram had hoped to achieve. Everyone seemed to be on good terms with everyone else and the rancour which had been roused by the behaviour of Dawn and Roger during the evening in San Juan had been dissipated.

At Tortola, one of the largest and most populated of the islands in the British group and which, even as late as the nineteenth century, had been a hideout for pirates, Mr Ingram had again taken the men of the cruise party on another tour of a new hotel and, as on St Thomas, Miranda had gone with them to take notes.

Now, at this smaller island, which was in the process of being developed in the way that Mr Ingram envisaged Fortuga being developed if only Transmarine could buy the whole of the Gallant estate, they were just returning from an extensive tour of building sites.

As she walked along behind the men on their return to the yacht Miranda thought there was no denying the relationship between Roger and Thomas even though they were so different in their ways. Thomas was still a handsome

65

man and he possessed the same graceful length of limb and the same elegant bone structure in his face as Roger. His thinning hair, however, was a light brown and his eyes were faded blue, like Chuck's. A few years ago he must have been very attractive, but too much high living had caused him to put on weight and now he looked full-blown, about to go to seed.

At every hotel site he had been an enthusiastic spectator and also here, on this small island. Determined to see that his younger cousin was as impressed as himself, he exclaimed at everything and occasionally took Roger's arm and drew his attention to something. Roger, on the other hand, had maintained a vague, almost flippant attitude. The two other men, Ramon and Chuck, had looked at everything reluctantly, obviously wishing they could be elsewhere.

'There's only one way to cool off after a tour of inspection in the heat of the day and that's to go swimming,' said Chuck, falling back to wait with Miranda. 'You know, I reckon that song of Noël Coward's is right. Only mad dogs and Englishmen would go out in the midday sun to do what we've just done, and there were far too many Englishmen around today. Those with latin blood in their veins, like Ramon and me, prefer a siesta on a day like this. Do you think Roger was impressed this time?'

'It was hard to tell,' she replied.

'Elusive guy, isn't he? I wonder where he's gone now? I asked him to come swimming with us, but as usual he had some vague excuse, as he's had every afternoon this week. I can't understand him. The underwater life in this particular group of islands is fabulous and I thought he'd like to come snorkelling. He's as cool a fish under the water as he is above it. Swims and dives with the best. But I guess he's found something better to do. How soon can you get changed?'

'Immediately,' said Miranda willingly, longing to cool off, and went down to her cabin.

There on the chest of drawers the conch shell shone with a mysterious pink glow. She shed her sticky clothing, had a quick shower and slipped into her new blue bikini. By now she was used to appearing almost naked in front of the others and her skin was developing a faint golden-pink tan, although she had still to take care that she didn't burn.

Putting on the white hat which Roger had given her, she thrust her feet into rope-soled sandals and pulled on a short thigh-length terry-towelling jacket. She collected her beach bag, which contained her towel and sun-lotion, left the cabin and padded along the passage.

The yacht was quiet. She guessed that Juanita and Ramon were having their usual siesta. Mrs Ingram would also be resting. Mr Ingram would be in his office planning and scheming. Did he ever rest? she wondered. He must be very pleased with the way everyone was behaving.

Although she herself had found it impossible, because of her innate shyness, to approach Roger deliberately, a friendship was growing between them as a result of his appearance every morning to share her moments on the sun-deck before breakfast in order to watch either the arrival or the departure of the yacht. On those strangely magical occasions he had been the same pleasant, amusing and informative companion who had shared the taxi with her in San Juan. . Once or twice, remembering what Mr Ingram expected of her, she had tried to boost Transmarine's hotels and point out the advantages to Fortuga of the Holding company's interest in the island, but on finding that he immediately withdrew or skilfully changed the subject, she soon gave up, preferring to listen rather than talk, making the most of having him to herself.

That was the only time she had shared with him, for he had a tendency to go off on his own in the afternoons and in the evenings the other members of the party were always about.

She saw much more of Chuck and it was with him that she had taken her first swim in the warm buoyant water of the Caribbean Sea; with him she had gone beachcombing; with him she had danced in the few night-spots they had visited during the course of the cruise; and now he was taking her snorkelling.

He was waiting for her by the gangway dressed in black swimming shorts, with a towel around his neck. He gave her an admiring glance as she joined him and put a friendly arm about her shoulders as they moved off along the curving stone wall of the dock.

'There's a little lagoon the other side of that promontory,' he said. 'We should be able to reach it by climbing through the bushes.'

They scrambled over the rocks. At the foot of them the sea broke in a flurry of lace-edged waves. Amongst the bushes were scattered shells of various sizes which caught Miranda's attention and caused her to stop.

'You can comb the beach on your way back,' urged Chuck. 'Come on!'

She hurried up the gentle slope to join him and together they began to walk down the other side. Through the foliage of the bushes and palm trees she could see glinting bone-white sand curving beside smooth blueish-green water. A few more steps forward and her view of the beach was widened and included several articles; a woman's white beach bag, two coloured towels carelessly tossed down; then two bodies, bronzed and glistening, naked except where the formality of bikini and brief swimming shorts covered them. They were in close embrace, reddish-brown hair contrasting strongly with silvery blonde tresses.

'Oh, no!' gasped Miranda, and looked away. She wanted to turn and run, but her legs felt strangely leaden.

'Now we know where he's been spending his afternoons,' said Chuck softly. 'That's why Pop is worried.'

'We must go somewhere else to swim,' murmured Miranda.

'No, we don't. We break it up before one thing leads to another,' asserted Chuck.

Without waiting to see if she would go with him he scrambled down the slope and as he went he called out derisively:

'Peekaboo, I see you two! Come on, you fellers, run for it. If you don't want to be covered by sand, get in that lagoon!'

Roger raised his head. He saw Chuck advancing, kicking up sand, and he sprang to his feet. He ran towards the sea with long strides of shapely golden brown legs. Like wing-footed Mercury, he was a muscular, elegantly shaped man in the briefest of white swimming shorts, sprinting over the sand. Right out into the water he ran sending up a shower of sun-shot spray. He raised his arms above his head, and his powerful shoulder muscles rippled beneath his skin. His body curved and he disappeared, plunging into the smoothly rolling, scintillating surface of the water.

Deserted by her gallant, Dawn was trying to protect herself from the handfuls of sand which Chuck was throwing in her direction. She shrieked wildly at him as she held her hands in front of her face.

'Oh, you're hateful!' she yelled. 'I was having a great time, soaking up the sun, and you had to come and spoil it.'

'I bet you didn't think *he* was spoiling your great time,' jeered Chuck, jerking his head in the direction of Roger, who had surfaced several yards out and was swimming strongly, with brief flashes of sun-bronzed arms.

Dawn flung back her curling silver-gilt hair, leaned back on her elbows and looked up at her stepson.

'So that's what's bothering you, baby,' she drawled insolently. 'Going to tell your daddy? It's time you grew up, baby boy, and stopped telling tales. Ouch!' Chuck had kicked her lightly on the leg with his toes.

'Just watch your step with Roger,' he threatened unpleasantly, 'or there'll be real trouble between him and Pop, which is what we're all doing our best to avoid. If you don't, I'll make you sorry you ever gave Roger the come-hither looks you've been sending in his direction lately. Don't think for one moment that they haven't been noticed.'

'Think I can't handle two Gallants at once?' Dawn retorted. 'Or even three?' she added provocatively, her glance roving suggestively over his big shoulders and wide chest where a silver medallion glinted, hung from a chain around his neck.

'I think you can't handle that particular Gallant.' Again Chuck jerked his head in the direction of Roger.

'Which is why I've always found him exciting, perhaps,' retorted Dawn. Her glance flickered to Miranda. 'My you're still pale, aren't you?' she drawled disparagingly. 'You're not used to the sun, I suppose, and you're thin-skinned too. You'll look like a boiled lobster this evening if you're not careful and stay out too long today. Nothing looks worse than a red and peeling skin.'

With a lithe twist of her body she stood up and dashed off to the water. Her body arched and she also disappeared below the surface. Soon they saw her appear again and swim after Roger, going almost as strongly as he was.

Glancing at Chuck, Miranda saw that he was staring after the two people in the water. There was an oddly malevolent expression on his face. A heavy frown caused his thick dark eyebrows to meet almost above the bridge of his prominent nose. His eyes were narrowed to slits and his mouth had an unpleasant twist to it. With his swarthy skin and hawk-like features he reminded her of a picture she had once seen of a proud but vengeful conquistador gloating over the land and people he had just conquered, and she shivered.

He turned and grinned at her and at once the image was destroyed. He was Chuck again, a rather lazy but good-humoured young man who liked nothing better than to swim and surf in the sea and loll about in the sun.

'Dawn is furious because we interrupted them, so she took it out on you. But she's right, you'll have to take care not to

70

burn today. Let's sit down and I'll rub the lotion on your back. I wonder how long those two have been meeting together in the afternoons?' he said.

Miranda wondered too, although she did not want to consider the matter at all. Chuck's big hand was gentle and yet impersonal as he rubbed oil on her shoulders and he was still spreading it when Roger came out of the sea, tall and graceful, his hair like reddish-brown seaweed, the smooth curves of his tanned chest and shoulders glistening with water as he stood for a moment and watched.

Then he touched the snorkelling equipment with one bare foot.

'Where did you find this?' he asked.

'On the yacht. There's diving equipment too and a sailing dinghy. We could sail tomorrow if you'd like to help me rig it,' said Chuck.

'Could do. Who's going snorkelling now?'

'Miranda and I.'

'How far can you swim, Miranda?' Roger's voice had lost its lazy indifference and was sharp. She glanced up at him. He was still watching Chuck smooth her right shoulder with oil and there was a funny little twist at the corner of his straight firm mouth.

'I don't know. I'm not sure,' she replied.

'A length or two lengths of a normal swimming pool?' he persisted.

His question brought to mind the swimming pool where she swam sometimes in her lunch hour with her friends from the office in London. The bottom of the pool had been painted bright blue to give the water the colour of the tropical sea and on the tiled wall of the hall palm trees had been painted. It was a far cry from this idyllic lagoon on a real tropical island.

'I think I can swim about four hundred yards,' she said.

'Have you ever swum under water?'

'No, not properly.'

'Then I suggest that you should practise first, before us-

71

ing the snorkel. The lagoon is more sheltered further along, over by that other headland. You go and get some more equipment, Chuck, and I'll take Miranda for a practice swim to see that she comes to no harm.'

Chuck's indrawn breath was audible and he let it out with a deliberate explosion.

'Of all the barefaced cheek!' he seethed, looking suddenly very like his father. 'You go and get the equipment and I'll take Miranda for the practice swim. You seem to have forgotten that this afternoon you've got someone your own age and weight to play with, as you've had every afternoon this week, I expect.'

He glanced at Dawn, who was just coming out of the sea. With her silvery hair glittering with drops of water, her smooth, full-bosomed, tiny-waisted figure glistening, she appeared like some mermaid waiting to lure men to their destruction.

Roger smiled as he looked at Chuck, that faint enigmatic curving of his mouth.

'Could it be that you're jealous?' he queried softly, then stepped back as Chuck stood up and swung a fist at him. 'All right. Tell me where the equipment is and then all four of us can go snorkelling.'

Chuck suppressed his irritation and explained briefly where the equipment could be found and Roger turned at once and was soon climbing up the rocks.

'It doesn't matter what anyone says to him, he never gets riled,' marvelled Chuck, who was still angry. 'If he'd said to me what I said to him, I'd have blown my top and hit him.'

'You nearly did,' remarked Dawn, coming up to them. 'Where has he gone?'

'To hide from you,' retorted Chuck nastily. 'Come on, Miranda, let's go to the other end of the beach.'

The water was clear and deep in the lagoon. Being protected from the open sea, it was ideal for swimming and diving. For a while Miranda and Chuck swam, and when he was satisfied she could swim far enough under water without the snorkel, he showed her how to use it, helped her fit the flippers to her feet, fixed the mask over her eyes and nose and did the same for himself. Together they waded out into the middle of the pool, and soon were swimming under the glittering surface.

Below was a cool, translucent world where pretty plants waved their long fronds amongst stems of white coral. Schools of small tropical fish, silver and sapphire, gold and emerald, swam in and out of the plants and the pale flat sand was scattered with colourful shellfish of all shapes and sizes.

When they returned to the beach they found Dawn sitting there alone. She was smoking a cigarette in quick nervous puffs and she was looking sulky.

'Roger hasn't come. What you say to him?' she demanded petulantly of Chuck.

'I told him where to find the snorkelling equipment and he said he'd go and fetch some more so that he and you could snorkel too,' replied Chuck easily. 'Maybe he couldn't find it.'

'You said more than that,' attacked Dawn. 'You said something he didn't like, so he hasn't bothered to come back. You're a damned nuisance, and even though you look like your mother you have the Gallant knack of poking your nose in where it isn't wanted, baby boy. Just like Marnie did—and remember what happened to her.'

'Never mind, Dawn,' he said soothingly, although his face darkened with anger again. 'You're not going to be alone for long. Here comes your other admirer.'

There was a warning note in Chuck's voice and both Miranda and Dawn turned to look along the beach. Doug Ingram was approaching them. He was wearing a beach outfit, dark red swimming shorts and a loose jacket to match, unbuttoned to show his thickly-muscled chest. Relieved to see him, because the bickering between Chuck and his stepmother was beginning to alarm her, Miranda was glad to see that Mr Ingram's skin was quite as pale as her own. In his hand he was carrying two sets of flippers and two snorkelling masks.

'I ran into Roger,' he explained. 'He said you were down here.' He was looking down at Dawn and smiling at her. 'This is a wonderful spot, but Thomas tells me that the lagoon on Fortuga is even better. Is there anything interesting below the surface?'

Miranda dutifully described what she had seen, noting that he wasn't really listening, but was eyeing Dawn out of the corner of his eyes. Aware that she was being eyed, Dawn suddenly lost her sulkiness, leaned back on her elbows as if she knew that in that position her seductive figure was shown off to advantage.

'I think I'll go and have a look for myself,' said Mr Ingram when Miranda had finished speaking. 'Like to come with me, Mrs Gallant?'

Dawn looked up at him slowly. Her eyes glittered provocatively in the sunlight as she looked him up and down.

'I'd love to, Mr Ingram,' she drawled.

She allowed him to help her with the equipment, although Miranda guessed that Dawn probably knew more about snorkelling than he did.

Chuck watched them go, flip-flopping over the sand to the twinkling water, with irritation marring his face. Then he began to collect equipment together.

'Let's go somewhere else to sunbathe,' he muttered.

They strolled back slowly along the beach and over the rocks. The sand was warm and soft between bare toes and after her swimming efforts Miranda felt pleasantly relaxed. It was such a beautiful place, shimmering almost-white sand, fringed by tall palms on one side, edged by gold-shot aquamarine-coloured water on the other.

'I wonder what your boss is up to,' said Chuck suddenly. 'Obviously he's the reason why Roger didn't return.'

'I wonder,' murmured Miranda, non-committally, pretending she wasn't startled by his remark which shattered

74

her peaceful lazy mood, bringing as it did to mind Mr Ingram's idea to use Dawn to bring pressure to bear on Roger to sell Gallant's Fancy.

This time when they climbed over the rocks they paused to collect shells. Miranda had quite a collection in her cabin now, all arranged round the conch shell. In a bookshop she had found a guide to the kind of shells to be found in the Caribbean and was now able to recognise a few of them. Their various shapes were fascinating—salmon pink cones, mottled spindles, delicately-spined murex, purple sea-snails and sundials, turbans and star-shells.

Finding a suitable place on the next beach near some palms, they stretched out in the sun and talked. It was a pleasant way to spend an afternoon and she had done it now several times with Chuck, although talking with him did not have the same magic as a conversation with Roger because Chuck was more interested in the future of Chuck Gallant than in anyone or anything else.

Like Juanita he had spent his early years on Fortuga before being taken to San Juan when his mother had left his father, but unlike Juanita he had chosen to finish his education in the States rather than in Britain. He hoped to qualify eventually as a lawyer and to return to Puerto Rico.

Today, however, by careful questioning, Miranda managed to get him to talk a little about Roger and Marnie.

'They're different from Nita and me,' he said. 'Their mother was from England and they were sent to private schools in England. With their pukka English accents and their funny little loyalties and self-discipline they often strike me as being more English than the English. Then I see Roger behaving as he was with Dawn this afternoon and I begin to wonder about him. Perhaps the passionate latin blood which runs in the family stirs in him occasionally too.'

'Or perhaps he's been too long in the sun,' murmured Miranda lazily, thinking she must move soon because she felt as if she had been too long in the sun that day.

'What do you mean?' Chuck's voice was nearer. She opened her eyes and saw him leaning over her, a dark stranger.

'Before coming here I was told that I'd most likely meet people who looked English and talked English, but I mustn't expect them to behave like the English people I know because they and their ancestors had lived here too long in the sun. Now I've been here and have seen the effect the day's sunshine has on everyone, I understand better what that means,' she replied.

'I know too,' said Chuck. 'A day spent under the tropical sun relaxes the inhibitions. Has it relaxed yours, Miranda?'

His voice had softened and there was a fire aglow in his eyes which no longer seemed to be a faded blue. His mouth was full and red, sensual like his father's. Miranda did not want it to touch hers. She closed her eyes and tried to think of Joe, but all she saw was another mouth, firm yet sensitive. Roger's. If his mouth touched hers she wouldn't object.

She opened her eyes quickly, the only way to banish such wayward un-Miranda-like thoughts, the result surely of her having been too long in the sun that day.

'You're full of inhibitions too, aren't you?' Chuck scoffed gently, leaning closer. 'The sight of Roger and Dawn in each other's arms on the sand of a deserted beach this afternoon sent you into a state of shock almost.'

'Well, I must admit I'm not used to seeing people behaving with such abandon in full daylight in public, especially when one of them happens to be married to another person,' she retorted, wondering how she could manage to avoid being kissed by Chuck without upsetting him too much. How to be diplomatic in this situation was very much beyond her experience.

'In public?' he exclaimed. 'There's nothing public about a deserted sandy beach shaded by palms and lapped by the blue sea. In fact it's the most romantic place in the whole world. They were only kissing, Miranda. Like this.'

76

His mouth touched hers after all and she didn't object because to do so would be undiplomatic, but she kept her eyes open and gazed at the pattern made against the sky by the slotted leaves of the palm tree. To have closed her eyes would have been dangerous.

It was rather like being between the devil and the deep blue sea, she thought, although it was difficult to decide who was the devil—Chuck with his dark hair and swarthy face, who was actually kissing her, or the Roger of her imagination.

Her sense of humour suddenly got the better of her and laughter welled up. She spluttered, and Chuck sat up to glare down at her with furious eyes.

'What are you laughing at?' he demanded.

'You,' she giggled, forgetting all about diplomacy and behaving naturally. 'As Roger said, you were jealous of him this afternoon, weren't you? You were jealous because he seemed to be having all the fun. So you thought you'd do the same, and I happened to be handy. But it's no use, Chuck. I'm just not that sort of person. I can't play at love like some people. For me it's a very private and personal business. I don't like being kissed by a man just because it's the time of day to kiss and make love on the sands.'

He glowered at her, and she knew she had hurt his feelings.

'You're more than inhibited,' he growled. 'You're frozen. *You* haven't been long enough in the sun.'

Deciding that it would be better not to rise to his taunt, she stood up and picked up her beach bag.

'I'm going back to the yacht. I think I've sunbathed long enough. I have to write a letter before dinner to my boyfriend. I've only sent cards to him so far and he'll be expecting a letter.'

'O.K.' He was sulky now, like a small boy who had been deprived of something he wanted very much. 'So you've got a boy-friend back home. What else is new? Funny you didn't tell me about him before. I suppose he comes under

77

the heading of personal and private. I guess you're serious about him.'

'Yes. We're going to be married when I return to England,' said Miranda, suddenly seeing a way to avoid further amorous complications with Chuck.

'I see, then I'm sorry I took advantage,' he mumbled, still sulky, 'but you might have told me.'

The letter to Joe was more difficult to write than she had anticipated. In her cabin, hearing the water lapping against the side of the yacht and the sound of the early evening breeze rustling the leaves of the palms, seeing the pink of the conch shell gleaming at her, Joe seemed curiously unreal, a phantom dimly seen. She tried to imagine him there with her, walking on the sand that afternoon, swimming in the warm silken water, kissing her in the shade of a palm tree, and she couldn't.

So she tried something else. She tried to imagine him breakfasting with her under an awning on the sun-deck, escorting her through palm-shaded passages, fitting hats on her head and standing back to study the effect, buying her a conch shell and presenting it to her with a sincere little speech, and she couldn't.

He wouldn't fit in, and when she tried to measure him against the complex uninhibited members of the Gallant family he seemed rather dull and insignificant.

Miranda screwed the sheet of writing paper up and tossed it into the waste basket. She would try to write to-morrow morning when she felt a little calmer, when her pulse rate had slowed and her over-heated blood had cooled.

Dinner that night was a casual barbecue affair served on the beautiful crescent-shaped beach. The crew having been given the afternoon and evening off, Mr and Mrs Ingram did the cooking, turning sizzling slices of steak and ham over the smoking charcoal as if they'd been born to cook in that way.

Miranda stood by helping everyone to salad. When Roger came to be served she avoided looking at him. She had decided earlier that she didn't wish to have anything to do with someone who kissed other men's wives. After the little scene near the lagoon she had no doubt that he thoroughly deserved the reputation he had earned as a play-boy and a gallant in the broadest sense of the word. The Roger she had met in San Juan and had known in Charlotte Amalie she would keep tucked away in a hidden corner of her heart, but never again would she let herself be deceived into thinking he was someone with whom she could be friends.

As it was, he had nothing to say to her, and after taking some salad on his plate he strolled way into the shadows beyond the firelight, perhaps to sit with Dawn.

Juanita was there, in lively mood, bubbling over with enthusiasm about the flamingo pool which she and Ramon had found late that afternoon. Ramon teased her gently and lovingly and, watching them together, Miranda thought again of Joe and wondered whether such happiness would ever be theirs when they were married.

Her thoughts did not go far, because Doug Ingram was beside her talking in an undertone.

'You remember me saying that Mrs Gallant might be able to bring some pressure to bear on Roger?' he murmured.

Miranda nodded as she heaped his plate with salad.

'Well, I had a talk with the lady in question and she was only too pleased to fall in with my suggestions. Unfortunately she was seen with him in a rather compromising situation this afternoon by Chuck, and she's afraid he might tell her husband. It wouldn't do at all for Thomas to get wind of it, so you might take him in hand, if you please, make him feel comfortable, show him we're still interested in him. Zelda has been doing her best, but Thomas, like all the Gallants apparently, has a roving eye, and he likes his women friends to be young, if you know what I mean.'

'Yes, I know what you mean, Mr Ingram,' replied Miranda, feeling slightly sick. She wasn't sure whether it was the thought of Thomas Gallant's roving eye which caused the nausea to rise, or whether it was the thought of having to keep him entertained while his wife used her obvious attractions to persuade Roger to change his mind about selling Gallant's Fancy.

She didn't find it difficult to talk to Thomas, who seemed a little lost, his wife having disappeared into the shadows and Zelda Ingram being too busy entertaining the manager in charge of the development of the island and his wife, who were the Ingrams' guests for the evening. Thomas therefore was glad to unburden himself to Miranda and was disposed to tell her of the time he had held barbecue parties on the beach in Fortuga.

'It's a lovely place,' he boomed. 'Regular paradise. It tears me in half to have to sell my place, but I believe in progress. We can't live in the past all the time, and that's what we've been doing on Fortuga, we Gallants, still fancying ourselves as plantation owners and distillers of rum.'

'And pirates,' suggested Miranda rather cheekily. He laughed heartily.

'We'll always be that. Scratch any of us and underneath you'll find a pirate or a smuggler, for all we like to pretend we're civilised now. If you're interested in pirates you'd have liked my cousin Rupert, Roger's father. He and I shared a great-grandfather—a grand chap. We were the best of friends, when we weren't fighting, that is,' Thomas laughed again. 'He could have told you all about the pirates in the Gallant family. He was writing a history of Fortuga.'

'What happened to him?'

'It was a tragedy,' Thomas sighed heavily. 'He was a great seaman. Owned a big yawl. Used to sail it about the Caribbean like our pirate forebears. He crossed and re-crossed the Atlantic many times, just as if it were the English Channel. It was a great blow to me when he was drowned. He and his wife, Mary—she was a fine woman with roses in her cheeks and a gay smile—were sailing back to Fortuga from Trinidad with their eldest son Francis. Rupert had been there attending to various business concerns. They were caught in a bad storm. The yacht sank and they were all drowned. It was terrible. I could never understand how a seaman like Rupert could have let himself be caught out in a storm like that, but it happens to the best sometimes.'

'How long ago did it happen?' asked Miranda.

'Let me see now. Roger was fifteen at the time—it must be about sixteen years ago. It left me with him on my hands. Rupert had made me guardian in his will of any of his children who happened to be under age when he died.' Again Thomas's sigh was heavy. 'I wish he hadn't. I had all kinds of trouble with that scamp. You wouldn't believe the scrapes he used to get into, not only on Fortuga but at school in England too. Mischievous from the time he was born. Apple of his grandmother's eye just because he could sing a tune and make up songs. He tormented the life out of me and he still does. Mind you, I'm not saying he wasn't upset by the accident. He was, because he thought the world of his parents and his brother, but he had no interest in growing sugar cane or anything else. All that mattered to him was music.'

'What about Marnie?'

'She was old enough to look after herself and did just that. Clever girl, Marnie. She took a degree in chemistry. She might have taken Rupert's place in the distillery company, but there was that accident which blinded her, and that put paid to that. I sold out my shares and theirs to the highest bidder. You see, it wasn't the same without Rupert. He was the business man, and Francis was like him.' Thomas sounded on the defensive now. 'My only talent seems to be in choosing the wrong woman to be my wife.'

He sighed gustily again and looked around, peering into the shadows as if he could penetrate their gloom, obviously searching for Dawn.

Miranda exerted herself and led the conversation into other less uncomfortable channels and was glad when Mrs Ingram appeared to suggest that they all go on board and have drinks and possibly a game or two of cards. The plan was to leave early in the morning and motor down through the Leeward Islands.

Relieved to have a little time to herself, Miranda decided to take one more stroll along the beach. She would not pass that way again and she wished to remember it in the future as a place of perfect peace and beauty.

A sickle of moon was sliding down the sky and its rays turned the sand from pale ivory to silver. The leaves of the palms made dark shadows on the sand and at its edge the sea murmured perpetually, sometimes noisily with little rushes of sound, sometimes softly with a faint throbbing undertone. In its dark moving mass stars winked at their own reflection. *Stars in the Sea,* a sad little song of lost love with an unusual lilting melody almost like the sound of the sea tonight. Miranda wondered what incident had touched the depth of feeling which she guessed Roger Gallant hid beneath his careless and sometimes flippant exterior and had brought forth new and nostalgically beautiful music.

A shadow loomed behind her on the sand. She stopped walking and the shadow stopped too, remaining perfectly motionless. She began to walk again and it moved, following her, the distorted shape of a human head and shoulders.

Keeping her gaze on the shadow, wondering who was following her, she stopped again suddenly and it stopped too.

Miranda whirled round.

'Who are you? Why are you following me?' she demanded.

The moonlight picked out white trousers, glinted on a belt buckle and on the buttons fastening a dark shirt, highlighted the aquiline features of a face and found glints of silver in smoothly brushed hair.

'Just making sure you don't walk too far and fall into a

mangrove swamp,' Roger replied easily, coming towards her.

'Oh. Is there one?' cried Miranda, horror that she might have stepped into something unpleasant in the dark causing her skin to become clammy and cold.

'Yes. You were heading straight for it. It isn't always wise to walk in the dark on these islands when you don't know them. There are all sorts of hidden dangers.'

'You could have come and told me you were here instead of pretending you weren't,' she accused, recovering a little.

He laughed.

'I suppose I could have done, but I thought that perhaps you didn't want company. Sometimes it's necessary to be alone for a while, to catch one's breath and revaluate. I realise you must find living at such close quarters with members of the Gallant family a little trying, to say the least, and at times positively shocking.' There was a questioning lilt in his voice and it was still there when he added, 'And you were shocked this afternoon, weren't you, Miranda?'

Strangely confused because he had understood her reason for wanting to be alone, she answered stiffly, trying hard not to let herself be influenced by his friendly charm.

'Yes, I was.'

'And now you would rather not have anything to do with me any more?'

He was making a statement, but there was still that teasing questioning lilt. Five minutes ago when she had been alone that had been how she had felt about him, but now he was with her, close beside her in the warm scented darkness, she knew she could not agree with him. He had a fascination for her which would draw her to him no matter what he did.

'Perhaps you were carried away by the surroundings,' she said seriously, offering him an excuse. 'Chuck says there's no more romantic place in the world than a deserted beach under the tropical sun.'

'He was merely describing how such circumstances affect him,' he murmured, amusement threading the quiet lilt of his voice. 'As you discovered for yourself a little later in the afternoon.'

'You saw us?' she exclaimed, her cheeks growing warm at the thought of him seeing her being kissed by Chuck. How hypocritical he must think she was. 'He was only trying to be like you,' she blurted out defensively, feeling very foolish. 'It meant nothing.'

'Then why should you assume that my kissing Dawn meant something?' he returned blandly.

'I ... I ... don't know,' she confessed. 'It looked and seemed different. Besides, she's married to your cousin.'

'While you are only promised to be married, or so you say,' he taunted. 'A big difference, I agree. Dawn married Tom for his money when he had some. Now he's broke again and looking and feeling his age. She's young and talented, and would dearly like to leave him to move in with someone younger, wealthier, someone who's made the contemporary scene and on whom the limelight shines occasionally.'

'Yourself?' she accused.

'Exactly. At least that's how I'm interpreting her revived interest in me and her determination to seek me out in the afternoons and share in my daily worship of the sun.' There was a dryness in his voice which could not be ignored, and Miranda felt a tingle of alarm. Was he suspicious of Dawn? 'Of course she could have another reason,' he added. 'Am I to believe by the reproving tone in your voice that you don't like the idea of her leaving Thomas for someone else?'

'No, I don't,' she replied coolly.

'I suppose it doesn't appeal to your idealistic view of marriage as the happy ending to the gently conducted courtship,' he jibed lightly. 'If that's the case you're in for more shocks here under the tropical sun where physical attraction often flares up in response to the heat and the romantic setting and demands to be satisfied. You had a small experience of your own with Chuck this afternoon.'

'That isn't so,' she denied hotly. 'I'm not attracted to Chuck at all. I didn't like being kissed by him. I don't care to be kissed by a man who doesn't love me. I believe physical love to be the expression of a person's deepest feelings for another person. Without those deep feelings one shouldn't make love.'

'You're right, of course. One shouldn't, but one sometimes does,' he said drily. 'Why don't you like being kissed? Are you afraid you might find out something about yourself which doesn't fit in with that strict code of values your Aunt Clara had imposed upon you? Are you afraid you might discover you're a woman with a woman's real desires and not a strait-laced adolescent living in a dream-world half the time?'

He had come so near the truth that she could think of no answer. Her silence betrayed her and he laughed.

'Your Joe shouldn't have let you out of his sight,' he said. 'He should have married you out of hand instead of letting you come here. You won't be the same when you go back, you know. You'll have memories which will torment you.' He paused, then asked idly, 'What does he do, this safe and sound young man of yours?'

Glad that he had changed the subject slightly, Miranda answered readily:

'He's a builder.'

'Not of hotels, I hope,' he remarked.

'No, only houses. You didn't like the hotels we looked at on St Thomas and Tortola, did you?' she replied, doing her best to direct the conversation into safer channels.

'Did I make it obvious?' He sounded a little surprised.

'Yes. You looked thoroughly bored, and you were very rude to Mr Ingram.'

'I intended to be,' he retorted. 'He has a tough hide.'

'Perhaps you'll like the hotel on Grenada better,' she rushed on, determined to use this moment to further the interests of Transmarine as she had been instructed by Mr

85

Ingram. 'It's been designed to fit in with local architecture. It isn't a high-rise, but is built like a series of connected native huts about two storeys high, with thatched roofs arranged around courtyards where fountains play and fish swim in pools; with beautiful patios shaded by poinsettia trees and bougainvillaea. It can hardly be seen from the road or from the sea, it blends so perfectly with the landscape. Yet it has every modern convenience; a swimming pool and boutiques. I can hardly wait to see it.'

'Well done, Miranda,' he remarked ironically, and she stiffened. Was it possible he had guessed what she had been trying to do? 'You're to be admired for your loyalty to your boss as well as to your young man, even if you are beginning to sound like an advertising brochure. I'm sorry to have to tell you that you're wasting your breath. Nothing I see or hear of Transmarine's hotels or complete holiday resorts is going to change my mind about selling Gallant's Fancy.'

'But what will your cousin do?'

'He got himself into this mess, he can get himself out. I owe him nothing,' Roger said in a hard flat voice she scarcely recognised. 'Once he duped Marnie and me into parting with our shares in the distillery. I was under age at the time and she was out of the area, in England. This time I'm going to make sure he doesn't trick anyone. When you see Gallant's Fancy you'll understand why I feel the way I do. When you meet Marnie, my sister, you'll understand why I can't sell her home and take her to live in London or New York, or anywhere else.'

'How long has she been blind?' asked Miranda, impressed by the sincerity in his voice.

'About ten years.'

'Can nothing be done to cure her blindness?'

'No.'

'How did it happen?'

'There was an accident.'

She could tell by his curt answers that he disliked her

questions and had no wish to tell her more, so she withdrew immediately.

'I'm sorry,' she murmured rather stiffly.

'Thank you,' he replied, his voice softening a little as if he sensed she was hurt by his refusal to explain further. 'I'd like you and Marnie to meet. You have a lot in common with her. She also has a strong sense of loyalty and strong views as to what's right and proper, so strong that they're likely to stand in the way of her personal happiness.' He paused, then added inconsequently, 'I saw something else this afternoon which I believe I wasn't supposed to see. Your Mr Ingram is a smooth operator. It would be interesting to know what he was discussing so intimately with Dawn as they sunbathed together.'

Again Miranda stiffened, suddenly aware that there was an ominous difference in the atmosphere around them. The night air was heavy and humid. Both moon and stars had disappeared, obscured by cloud. The sand no longer scintillated and there were no shadows. The only light was that blazing from the yacht in the distance, where it was tied up to the wharf. She knew Roger was still there because she could hear him breathing and sense that his compact vibrant body was close to her.

Should she tell him that Mr Ingram hoped to use Dawn to persuade him to sell Gallant's Fancy and that that was the reason for her revived interest in him? Where did one's loyalty to one's employer begin and end? Would it hurt Roger to know the truth? Was it possible he was in love with Dawn?

Being the person she was, she was much more in sympathy with Roger now that she knew his reason for obstructing the purchase of the Gallant estate on Fortuga than she was with Mr Ingram. Confused, caught on the horns of a dilemma, she stood miserably silent, not knowing what to do.

'You know what they were discussing, don't you?' said Roger quietly, and she knew that he had stepped closer to her. 'Are you going to tell me?'

His voice was soft and persuasive and he was so near to her now that she could distinguish the clean wholesome smell of the soap he used to wash with from the more cloying, exotic scents of the island.

'I don't think I should,' she replied as coolly as she could.

'You don't *think*, but what do you feel? That's what really matters, isn't it?'

A hot wind, a mere zephyr fanning the cheeks, scarcely enough to lift the heavy palm leaves, wafting in off the quiet sea, touched Miranda as if to warn her of danger.

For the second time she felt anger beginning to simmer deep down inside her as she realised that Roger was very skilfully using his knowledge of her; knowledge gained during their few talks together. He had leaned that she disliked trickery and deceit and now he was playing on that dislike, hoping to make her divulge her knowledge of Mr Ingram's plans to trick him through using Dawn.

He had probably seen her come along the beach and had followed her with the intention of prising information out of her, just as he had once before in the taxi-cab in San Juan. He had disarmed her by talking about his sister. In a sudden revulsion of feeling she saw him as an enemy who had spied on her and Mr Ingram that afternoon.

Once again she did not wish to have anything to do with him. She wished to be as far away from him as possible; from his persuasive voice; from his taut elegant body, clothed now, but seen that afternoon in all its near-naked beauty; from his firm well-shaped mouth, no longer a figment of her imagination but there in reality, inches above her own as he leaned towards her and reiterated in a murmur she could hardly hear above the whisper of the waves at the edge of the sand and the sight of strengthening wind in the palms:

'Are you going to tell me, Miranda?'

Anger, plus the fear of her own body's strange reactions

to his nearness, made her brave.

'What will you do if I don't?' she challenged.

His laughter had a warm, genuine sound which made her long to laugh too, almost disarming her again.

'There's very little I can do. I've always considered myself too civilised to resort to brute force. I could give you a shake, perhaps.'

He put his hands on her shoulders. She could feel the edge of them against her skin where her sleeveless dress left the top of her arms bare. His grasp was light, tentative almost, and yet she had a feeling that if she tried to slip out of it those fingers would grip mercilessly.

He shook her gently.

'I very much doubt that you'll give in to such gentle torture,' he said laughingly. 'Circumstances being what they are, a deserted sandy beach overhung by whispering palms, perhaps I'd get more co-operation from you if I do something you don't like and kiss you.'

There was no time to duck or step sideways as his hands slipped up from her shoulders to encircle her throat. Held like that she could not even turn her head. She intended to keep her eyes open as she had done when Chuck had kissed her that afternoon, but she was unprepared for the effect Roger's mouth, cool and firm against hers, would have on her. Her eyes closed voluntarily. Her body lost all its stiffness and became soft and suppliant. An exquisite feeling which was half pain, half delight spread from her mouth downwards through her body and the desire to respond to his kiss was beyond her control.

The sound of rain spattering on the broad leaves of the palms, the feel of it, hard and pellet-like on her arms and head, shocked Miranda out of the lovely treacherous pleasure she was experiencing as Roger's lips persuaded her that there was nowhere she would rather be than on the beach of a tropical island being kissed by him. The wind had increased in strength and was flinging rain violently upon them, in a drenching downpour that would soon soak them.

Appalled at the way her body and senses had been about to betray her, Miranda pulled herself frantically away from Roger. She heard a strange flat sound, felt her hand in contact with a hard lean cheek and realised to her amazement that she had slapped him soundly, although she had no memory of intending to do so.

'That wasn't fair!' she cried, in a strange choked voice she hardly recognised as her own. 'You have no right to force yourself on a helpless female!'

'There's no such person as a *helpless* female,' he retorted laughingly. 'Witness the way you've just slapped me. As for it being fair, I warned you when we met that all's fair in love and war, and it's war to the hilt between me and Ingram. I shan't forget in a hurry that he tricked me into coming on this cruise. You know what lies behind his conversation with Dawn this afternoon and you're going to tell me, even if I have to keep you out all night.'

She tried to dodge past him, but he caught her by the hand and to her surprise twisted her arm behind her back.

'Oh, you beast!' she raged, kicking at his shins and feeling a rush of almost sadistic pleasure when her foot found its goal and she heard him swear. But no matter how she twisted she could not break free of his hold.

'I thought you said you didn't use brute force,' she flung at him breathlessly, no longer a placid young woman, but a lithe, writhing, angry creature, determined to be free.

'You started it by slapping me,' he retorted. 'And don't think for one moment I'll not fight back just because you're a woman. I believe in equality all the way.'

Around them the tropical storm tossed and whirled its way across the island, tearing at trees and bushes as if it would uproot them, rousing the sea to a ferment so that it no longer whispered but crashed in foaming frenzy in huge breakers which flooded the beach, sending swirling greedy water around the feet of the man and woman locked in a struggle for mastery.

Realising ruefully that no matter how she struggled she did not have the strength to break that inflexible hold on her wrist, Miranda went limp, hoping to catch him unawares and that in that moment she would be able to pull free and run back to the yacht.

His hand did not relax.

'A clever move, Miranda,' he said almost approvingly, 'but not clever enough. I'm too old a hand at horseplay to be caught like that.'

There was a sort of exultant laughter rippling through him as if he was enjoying the fight, and before she could stiffen and renew her struggles he caught her round the knees and flung her over his shoulder in a fireman's lift and began to hurry through the rain. Her hand now free, Miranda pummelled his back and kicked her legs, but nothing she did deterred him from his intention of carrying her somewhere, she couldn't guess where.

She could hear rain drumming on a tin roof. Roger set her down on her feet. She heard a door slam and knew that they must be in a building of some sort, possibly one of the derelict shacks she had noticed amongst the bush at the back of the beach. It smelt of must and mildew. The wind blew in at a broken window and loose shutters banged against the outside walls.

'And now, Miranda, tell me what Ingram has been cooking up with Dawn or we'll stay here all night,' said Roger in a softly threatening voice which still had the suspicion of a laugh in it.

'You can't keep me here,' she retorted, still breathless from the fight.

She moved stealthily away from him towards the broken window, which she could just make out in the gloom, an oblong of paler grey. He heard her movements and followed, taking her wrist in his hand.

'Yes, I can,' he replied calmly. 'When I was exploring this afternoon I looked in here. There's a bed in the corner, a little dilapidated, but clean and whole. We should be comfortable on it for the night.'

His hand tightened and he pulled her after him. Miranda tried to resist. He tugged harder and she had to follow him reluctantly.

'Sit down,' he ordered, giving her a gentle push. She sat down warily on a straw-filled mattress and he sat beside her, still holding her wrist. Against her thigh she could feel his, hard and warm, through the thin stuff of his pants.

She recalled the conversation she had had with Thomas only that evening. He had described Roger as a mischievous scamp who had been involved in all kinds of scrapes when a youth. Now she recognised that she was up against a master at this sort of prank. He had kidnapped her, in a way, and with her lack of experience in any kind of mischief she didn't stand a chance against his superior strength, quicker wits and his inflexible purpose to get information out of her.

'Now you can begin to tell me what Ingram has been plotting with Dawn,' he urged her quietly.

Miranda sat silent, the fire of rebellion dying within her. She was still secretly amazed at her own behaviour out there on the beach. What would Aunt Clara have thought of her diligent well-behaved Miranda if she could have seen her almost swooning with desire in a man's arms and then fighting the same man like a wildcat?

'Miranda,' Roger said softly, and his breath fanned her cheek. His hold on her relaxed slightly and his fingers began to caress the delicate skin on the inside of her wrist, where her pulse leapt unevenly. 'I shall kiss you again if you won't tell me,' he threatened, and the laughter was back in his voice, bubbling up, asking to be shared.

His kiss was a weapon she dared not brave. If he kissed her again she would not be responsible for what she did. He knew that and was using his knowledge of her to defeat her. Once more she had that curious feeling of being between the devil and the sea, but now she knew who the devil was.

'You devil!' she hissed, trying to pull away from him. His hand tightened painfully and she gasped.

'I'm no devil, just an ordinary man trying to protect someone I love, trying to preserve what's left of my inheritance from a gang of twentieth-century pirates and using any weapon that comes to hand,' he replied seriously. 'Tell me, please, Miranda. You know you want to.'

'If we don't return to the yacht what will they think when they know we've been out all night?' she quavered, trying to stall for time as much as she could.

'I don't really care what they think, but you can avoid any misunderstanding by telling me what I want to know. Once you've done that I'll take you straight back to the yacht. Tell me, Miranda.'

He had leaned towards her to whisper in her ear and his weight pushed her back against the wall. She felt his lips against her ear, then they moved along her cheek in a journey of exploration on their way to her mouth. She knew a sudden wild longing to let him continue with his gentle plundering, to stay silent and let him kiss her.

Then surprisingly she thought of Marnie, who was blind and whose home he was trying to preserve, and she started to speak in a low monotone.

'Mr Ingram is hoping that Dawn will be able to put some sort of pressure on you to sell Gallant's Fancy. I don't know the details of his plan.'

He moved away from her immediately and released her wrist.

'I was right, then.' The cold bleakness of his voice made her shiver. Was it possible he was disappointed to find that Dawn's interest in him was simulated after all? 'It seems that there's nothing that Ingram won't stoop to in order to pull off another of his grasping deals for Transmarine. He's even asked you to do what you can to persuade me to sell, hasn't he?'

'Yes,' she muttered. 'I didn't want to, and I'm not very good at doing what he suggested.'

'No, you're not,' he agreed, amusement back, warming his voice again. 'What did he suggest you do?'

'Be friendly towards you. Find out why you don't want to sell. Keep pointing out the advantages of Transmarine hotels and developments over those of other organisations. Do anything, except—except . . .'

'Except what?' He was sharp.

'He said that he didn't expect me to go beyond the bounds of propriety,' she said in a muffled voice, and this time his laugh was mirthless.

'How very kind and considerate of him,' he jeered. 'Did he say why he thought it a good idea to use you and then Dawn?'

She didn't answer, remembering Mr Ingram's initial assessment of Roger's character.

'Did he?' he prodded, moving close to her again.

'Yes,' she replied hastily. 'He said you were known to be susceptible to the charms of women.'

'Did you believe him?'

'I accepted his opinion. You see, until he asked for me to be sent out here to work for him and he wrote to me telling me about you, I'd never heard of you, so I didn't know whether you were or not. Was he right?'

He was quiet, apparently considering her question. Eventually he said slowly:

'Like Ferdinand in *The Tempest*, "Full many a lady have I eyed with best regard; and many a time the harmony of their tongues hath into bondage brought my diligent ear; for several virtues I have liked several women." He stopped and then added in a colder voice, 'But I should be slandering myself if I told you that I'd sell Marnie's home and my inheritance just to earn a woman's favour. Your boss's reading of my character was way out and probably based on hearsay and publicity. Do you understand?'

'Yes, oh yes, I do, but I'm sorry I can't tell you any more. I've really no idea how Mrs Gallant intended to put pressure on you.'

'You've told me enough,' he replied bleakly. 'I can guess the rest, and I don't like Ingram any the better for it. Now I'm forearmed and can deal with him as he deserves.'

There was a strange, springing steeliness in his voice which was new. It was as if a rapier had been unsheathed in readiness to fight a duel, and Miranda shivered again.

He felt her shiver and leaned forward.

'Thank you for telling me, Miranda,' he said gently. 'I'm sorry I've frightened you, but I had to know.'

His mouth brushed hers in the lightest of kisses and then he stood up and went across to the door. Limp and miserable, she leaned against the wall, reluctant to leave the kind darkness of the shack which had been the scene of her defeat. Rain was still drumming on the roof and when the door opened she could hear it swishing down.

'It isn't raining as hard as it was,' said Roger. 'Do you want to risk running to the yacht?'

She struggled off the bed and went over to look out, realising that staying there in the sheltering dark with him would finally be more dangerous to her than going out into the storm would be.

'I'll have to. I can't stay here with you any longer!' she cried in a queerly choked voice.

'Nor can I stay with you,' he retorted, on a note of suppressed violence.

He grasped her hand and together they ran down the slope through the clinging bushes on to the sodden beach. The wet sand sucked at their feet, making progress difficult, but Roger never stopped running and Miranda was pulled inexorably after him.

Beside the stone wall of the dock, bobbing up and down on the wind-whipped, storm-black water, *Sea Quest* was still ablaze with light. Breathlessly they ran along the dock in the slanting rain, pounded down the gangway and through the door into the brightly lit passage.

Mrs Ingram appeared in the entrance to the main saloon. She was in her dressing gown and she looked irritated. Her sharp suspicious gaze looked over the white-faced, wide-eyed young woman whose hair was a wild, wet tangle, whose soft mouth was a dark bruised pink and whose torn, bedraggled dress clung to her slim figure outlining every curve. It moved on with interest to the tall man with the dark red hair, whose eyes were hard and bright in his bronzed aquiline face and whose soaked clothing was plastered to his body, clinging to muscular shoulders and limbs.

'I was wondering what had happened to you Miranda,' she said sharply. 'It's past one o'clock and you know we want to make an early start. It was foolish of you to wander off so far. Doug would like to see you as soon as possible in the morning, when you will have to account for your strange behaviour. Where did you find her, Roger?'

'About to step into a mangrove swamp. We were forced to shelter from the storm or we would have returned earlier than this,' Roger replied smoothly. 'Better take a hot shower, Miranda. I'll bring you a hot rum toddy, if you like, to ward off any chill.'

'No, no, thank you,' she stammered wildly. Wrenching her hand from his grasp, she fled down the companionway and along the passage to her room. Once in the cabin she closed the door and locked it, as if by doing so she could lock out from her mind all that had happened to her that night on the beach.

CHAPTER FOUR

THE next morning was fresh and clear after the storm. A clean azure sky arched above an azure sea which was stippled with silver flecks as the crests of waves caught and reflected the sunlight and tiny flying fish leapt briefly into the air, a flurry of silvery movement above the surface before they dived below again.

Miranda, up early as usual, stood at the rails on the top deck of *Sea Quest* and watched the crescent of pale sand edged by palm trees and backed by green bush where she had experienced such an emotional upheaval the night before disappear into the blue distance.

She did not linger long because she had to go to Mr Ingram's office to report on her recent activities, and when she saw Roger, slim and elegant in cream pants and dark red shirt, approaching her, she turned and fled to the other side of the deck so that she did not have to meet him or speak to him. That would have to wait until her state of mind had returned to normal. She went into the main saloon and from there made her way to the cabin which was used as an office.

To her surprise and relief, Mr Ingram was smooth and pleasant, showing nothing of the displeasure which his wife had attributed to him the previous night. He went straight to the point, asking her if she had had any success in persuading Roger to consider selling Gallant's Fancy to Transmarine.

Thinking guiltily of how she had told Roger of Mr Ingram's scheming with Dawn, she answered honestly:

'No, I haven't.'

'I hope you didn't waste your time last night,' he said with a faint touch of exasperation. 'I thought it was a heaven-sent opportunity for you when he offered to go and

97

look for you and spent so much time with you.'

'I ... I ... tried to,' she stammered. Then suddenly resentment because he expected so much of her burst its bonds and she blurted, 'I can't do as you ask. It's impossible! I'm not that sort of person.'

He raised his eyebrows and the suggestion of a sneer curved his firm mouth.

'Finding him too hot to handle, are you?' he guessed shrewdly.

Miranda's cheeks flamed, but she managed to return his gaze steadily.

'I don't want to have anything to do with him,' she replied.

'Very well. I can't say I'm pleased. In business personal feeling should be put aside if one is going to be successful, but perhaps you're too young and unsophisticated to understand that. We'll leave Roger to Mrs Gallant's more experienced approach. Now I'd like to spend some time this morning catching up on correspondence. After visiting the islands of Anguilla, St Kitts and Nevis, I'd like to spend a couple of days in Antigua. There should be mail from head office waiting for us there, including some from your family, I expect.'

The thought of letters from Aunt Clara and Dottie and possibly from Joe cheered Miranda and she went to work feeling much more lighthearted, glad to be rid of the responsibility of pretending to be friendly with Roger when her feelings concerning him were in such confusion.

The next five days, spent lingering amongst the Leeward Islands, followed the same pattern as the week spent in the Virgin Islands. Contrary to Miranda's expectations Chuck's discovery of Dawn and Roger kisssng on the beach had not shattered the atmosphere of confidence and trust which Mr Ingram had been to such pains to build up between Roger and Thomas and himself, and she could only assume that Chuck had not carried tales to his father after all.

Sightseeing, swimming and sunbathing were still the pattern of every day. Occasionally Mr Ingram held discussions with Roger and Thomas, but although there were no violent disagreements at those meetings, neither was any progress made, mostly because of Roger's deliberately vague and flippant manner when it came to discussing the future of Fortuga and his refusal to commit himself in any way.

Miranda had expected him to leave the yacht after learning of the way Mr Ingram had used Dawn to influence him. She had also expected him to steer clear of his cousin's wife. But to her surprise and dismay he gave Dawn more and more obvious attention. They did everything together and seemed to enjoy each other's company. All Miranda could find in favour of their interest in each other was that it made it easier for her to avoid Roger.

It was while they were in Antigua, that leaf-shaped island of hundreds of beautiful beaches, a yachtsman's paradise, where the flat fields of sugar-cane were dotted with dozens of old windmills, that Dawn and Roger disappeared together on the second morning.

Nothing was said about their absence by the others as they wandered about the restored dockyard where Lord Nelson's fleet had fitted out during the Napoleonic wars. Nothing was said either when they did not turn up for lunch at a very British stone-walled pub-styled restaurant, or when they failed to spend the afternoon swimming from the restaurant's private beach.

But when the sudden tropical darkness fell and they still had not returned, Thomas began to show signs of restlessness and refused to accompany the rest of the party to the Son et Lumière performance of the island's history which took place in the old dockyard and which they watched from a hill on the opposite side of the harbour. He said that he would wait on board the yacht in case the missing couple came back.

By dinner time Thomas was in a definitely quarrelsome mood and was inclined to blame Doug Ingram for the continued absence of his wife. Since Mr Ingram had hoped to leave Antigua soon after midnight in order to reach Martinique as early as possible the next day, he was also showing signs of irritation as time passed by.

They came at last just after midnight, driving up to the wharf in one of the island's taxi-cabs. They came aboard noisily, obviously in the highest of spirits and very pleased with themselves. They had been, they said, to see one of Roger's friends, a well-known jazz pianist who was performing for the season in a cabaret at one of the island's new super hotels. There was no doubt that Dawn had enjoyed her jaunt with Roger, and Thomas looked daggers at his smiling bright-eyed cousin before taking his wife off to their cabin, presumably to tell her of his disapproval of her desertion of him for a whole day.

Next day Miranda was up early as usual to keep a rendezvous with the island of Martinique as it appeared out of the morning haze. She could see mountains, dark blue against the eastern sunlight, seeming to float on the shimmering sea. Even at a distance the beautiful contours of the island were compelling and as the yacht approached nearer to it she could see that the most northerly mountain was barren and eroded where great streams of molten lava had poured down it, searing the earth and torturing and massacring almost thirty thousand people earlier in the century. For the mountain was Mont Pelée, one of the most destructive volcanoes of all time.

A movement to her left caught Miranda's attention and she stiffened, ready to move quickly to the other side of the yacht and make her escape should it be Roger, but it was only one of the crew making his way to the wheelhouse, so she relaxed again.

Her attempts to avoid Roger had been fairly successful because since that morning when they had left the Virgin Islands and she had so obviously turned her back on him he had made no further attempts to join her on deck in the early morning and during the rest of the days he had been too busy with Dawn.

100

Miranda found it difficult to explain to herself the reason for wishing to avoid him. She tried to pretend that it was because she disliked him, but she knew that wasn't true. It would be nearer the truth to say she was afraid of him because he had disturbed the person who was Miranda Benson and had brought to life another Miranda, a woman who could slap and kick, who could wrestle with a man with all the abandon of a virago yet whose body melted into surrender when he kissed her; a Miranda she had not known existed until that dark stormy night on a crescent-shaped beach.

She sighed, glanced along the deck too late. Roger was up early after all and was coming towards her, quiet-footed in his rope-soled espadrilles. His tailored shorts revealed the symmetry of bronzed muscular legs and a clinging knit sports shirt emphasised the straight line of his shoulders. He was without his sun-glasses for once, and his narrowed eyes glinted with green light as he looked at her.

He leaned golden-brown forearms on the rail and looked out at the island. His bare elbow touched hers and she flinched away, sliding along the rail, putting a few inches between herself and him for safety.

He looked over his shoulder at her and the curve of his mouth was sardonic.

'Are you going to run away as you've been running every time I've come near you recently?' he taunted. 'There's no need. I'm not going to try and get any information out of you, if that's what you're afraid of.'

His taunting mood jarred on her, destroying her pleasure in the morning.

'No, I'm not afraid of that. I just don't want to have my morning spoilt,' she countered. 'It was perfect until you came.'

He laughed, his eyes glimmering with amusement between short dark lashes. Laughter chased away the lines under his eyes and the hollows in his cheeks, relics of his roistering with Dawn the previous day.

'Trying out your claws?' he mocked. 'You'll have to do better than that if you want to scratch me. I've been hardened in a tough school by women who've excelled in feline remarks.'

Regret for those other mornings they had shared side by side at the rail welled up in Miranda. She hated him suddenly, with an intensity which shocked her because she had never felt hate towards anyone in her life before. She hated the perfect symmetry of his profile, the muscular grace of his body, all designed to catch the attention of any woman. She hated the slightly raffish air which was imprinted on him this morning, which only served to remind her how he had spent the day before, with Dawn, and seemed to make him subtly more interesting. He had no right to stand there and deliberately spoil her memory of the morning she had spent with him in St Thomas and to cheapen it with jeering remarks, intended to hurt her.

'I hate you!' To her surprise she spoke the words and they seemed to hang between them like a cloud of evil smoke, polluting the pristine clarity of the morning air.

'You're not very original. It's been said before,' he remarked cynically, and she remembered Dawn throwing the remains of her drink at him and saying that she hated him. Immediately she was angry with herself for behaving no better than Dawn.

His gaze grew sharply speculative as it lingered on the soft curves of her cheeks which the kiss of the sun had tinted with the exquisite colour of a tea-rose, golden-pink.

'I have to admit it hasn't been said with such passionate intensity before,' he added gently, and watched curiously as the tea-rose glow deepened as she reacted to his shrewdness.

His refusal to be angered by her remark frustrated her. Did he never lose his temper? Even when they had fought on the beach he had not been angry.

'I mean it. I never say what I don't mean,' she riposted clumsily, unused to the rapier-sharp give and take of sophisticated bantering. 'I hate you because—oh, because ...'

She saw that if she told him why she hated him he would have a new weapon to use against her, so she stopped and glared at him, her slight breasts rising and falling under the blue cotton shirt she was wearing, her eyes dark and troubled, the colour of the sea when a storm threatens.

'Because I kissed you,' he finished for her, still gentle. 'Because I wakened you from your innocent dream of love to the pleasures of reality. It had to happen some time. Better before your wedding day than on it, so that shock doesn't spoil what should be the happiest day of your life. Your Joe hasn't been courting you properly, Miranda. Does he really expect you to marry him knowing nothing?'

Shock and hate flared up in a final burst of flame, and all because he had learned more about her when he had kissed her once than anyone had learned about her in twenty-one years. Yet she knew nothing of him. Just as she thought she knew him and had grasped the essential Roger Gallant, he changed mercurially.

'I'm well aware of the facts of life,' she retorted furiously. His glance was indulgent as it slid over the shining smoothness of her hair and rested briefly on the soft pink of her mouth which was innocent of lipstick, unconsciously tempting.

'Oh, what a dull way to describe the natural instincts of human beings,' he murmured. 'If you were my betrothed I'd make sure you didn't go on your honeymoon so untutored in the language of love.'

My betrothed. The old-fashioned English word appealed to her. It was much gentler, more loving than the French fiancée. In a flash she saw what it would be like to be the betrothed of Roger Gallant, to be loved by him and wooed by him, with laughter as well as with ardour; to be taught the language of love by him until she had learned its mystery and was able to match his passionate words and gestures with those of her own.

But he was not her betrothed. Anguish because he was not and never would be crept up on her unawares and she

103

caught her breath sharply, turning away from him so that he might not see the expression on her face.

'Have I trespassed too far?' he asked. 'Is it possible that I'm right and there hasn't been any courting between you and the safe and sound Joe?'

She was silent and unmoving and once more her silence betrayed her.

'Then why the hell are you going to marry him?' he exploded. The violence of his words startled her. It belonged to the storm-dark night and a shabby hut in the Virgin Islands and not to this lovely calm morning off the coast of Martinique.

'Yes, you have gone too far,' she retorted, swinging round to face him. 'My personal life is none of your business. After all, I hardly know you.'

'We've known each other for years, Miranda,' he said softly, and she glanced at him wearily, disturbed by this suggestion.

'In a few weeks I'll be back in London and all this and you will be just a memory,' she faltered.

'To keep you awake at nights,' he murmured. 'I go to London often, spend more of my time there than on Fortuga now. I have a flat there. We could meet. London has its romantic spots no less than the Caribbean Islands.'

Miranda stared at him, searching his face for clues, fearful of the intention which she suspected lay behind his suggestion, imagining what might happen at the flat if she went there to meet him, but his eyes were unrevealing, shimmering green in the sunlight.

'No, I couldn't meet you. It wouldn't be right,' she declared desperately. 'I don't want to have anything to do with you.'

'Because of what Ingram has said about me? Because of Dawn?' he accused, suddenly bitter. 'If I told you why . . .'

'I don't want to hear!' she cried, interrupting him. She began to move away, but his hand on her arm stopped her.

'Don't run away, Miranda,' he said more gently. 'I promise I'll behave myself and not tease you any more.'

She looked at him and he smiled at her, albeit a rather weary facsimile of his usual smile.

'Look,' he said, pointing to the island, 'we're near enough now to see the remains of St Pierre, which was once called the Paris of the Caribbean. There's the tower of one of the cathedrals. It reminds me of a story I heard about one of the survivors of the disaster. He was the organist in that church and he was practising on the organ when the volcano erupted. He took shelter under his instrument and lived to tell the tale. The story appeals to me because I like to think he was saved by his love of music.'

The story diverted Miranda from her intention, as he had known it would, and she stayed beside him. Listening to him telling her more about the catastrophe she glanced over the shimmering water at the small toy-like buildings strung out along the shoreline beneath the towering mountain. Her glance travelled up the ravaged runnelled slopes of the mountain to the crater at the top. It was the canker of the beautiful island and it had stained the place with grief.

She looked sidelong at her companion. In the clear morning light his handsome face was shadowed and rather drawn. She remembered he had once described himself as being stained with grief, calling it his canker. What had caused that grief? The loss of his parents when he had been at a vulnerable age? The blinding of his sister, which for some reason lay on his conscience? There had also been mention of someone called Josephine. Who was Josephine and what had she done to add to his grief? And was that grief the reason why he sometimes spoke and behaved outrageously?

'The calamity had a very special effect on the temperament and personality of the people of the island,' he was saying. 'It instilled urgent and different values in their children and their children's children. Overnight they became aware of the fragile uncertainty of living beside a gigantic firework which might go off at any moment. As a result the people of Martinique really know the meaning of the expression *joie de vivre* and their god is *l'amour, toujours l'amour.'*

He slanted an amused glance at her and she knew, with a strange breathless anticipation, that he wasn't going to keep his promise not to tease her any more.

'Perhaps you won't like Martinique because you're afraid of love,' he mocked.

Miranda tilted her chin, trying to adjust quickly to his mercurial change of mood and to take in her stride his teasing.

'That isn't true. I'm not afraid of love.'

'Yes, you are,' he persisted. 'You're afraid of love which reaches out rejecting all restrictions and rules, which prompts you to break contracts and promises, which tempts you to behave naturally and impulsively and obey your instincts.'

She caught her breath again and began to back away from him, but he followed her.

'I could understand,' he continued, 'if you were one of those cold career women, but you're not. You're quiet and gentle, with hidden fires, a passionate innocent like that other Miranda, a girl to come home to, not just at the end of the day but at any time of the day or the night.'

'Stop! Please, Roger. You mustn't say things like that,' she pleaded. 'I'm going to marry Joe.'

The sun was hot on her face and head. It was time to be moving into the shade, to put on a sun-hat and sun-glasses, to rub protecting lotion on her skin.

'All right,' he said, and bitterness was back. 'Play it safe. Go back to England and marry him and be safe for the rest of your life. I only hope you won't regret it.'

This time he moved away from her, going across to the other side of the deck. She didn't follow him but went quickly along the side deck, through a door, in from the heat of the sun to the coolness of air-conditioning to have breakfast with Juanita and Ramon.

106

Later in the morning the yacht tied up at a wharf in a corner of the wide natural harbour, not far from the principal town of Martinique, Fort de France. All the men seemed to have individual interests to pursue, so after having made arrangements to meet for lunch Mrs Ingram, Dawn and Miranda set off, with Juanita, who spoke French almost as fluently as she spoke Spanish, to do the communicating and interpreting for them. The aim was to visit the shops to search for the perfumes for which the island was famed, and also to buy hand-printed cotton, designed and made by local craftsmen.

As the taxi-cab they had hired manoeuvred through the busy streets Miranda was surprised to see French *gendarmes* in their pale khaki uniforms and their hard, black peaked hats, directing the traffic through what was obviously a busy industrial centre, and she learned from Juanita that the island was in fact still a *département* of France.

Wandering along narrow streets lined with pleasant boutiques, which offered both local and French wares for sale and where flowers, purple, yellow and scarlet, tumbled in profusion down white walls from high black iron balconies, they found their way to an open-air market set out on the banks of a wide inlet of the sea which seemed to separate one part of the town from the other.

In this market tall graceful dark-skinned women, some of them wearing the brightly coloured *madras* turbans and long skirts typical of the older Martiniquaises and some dressed in more contemporary styles, presided over heaps of oranges, grapefruits and limes, whose clear crisp colours contrasted vividly with the deeper stronger reds and greens of peppers and tomatoes.

The market spread over the narrow bridge which spanned the inlet. On the other bank sturdy open fishing boats painted bright blue and orange nuzzled the shore while fishermen and their families offered fish for sale, fresh from the sparkling waves of the Caribbean Sea.

The heat of the day eventually caused them to turn back

to the main square, to the pavement café where they had arranged to meet the men. There they were glad to sit on white-painted wrought iron chairs, to sip cool iced drinks and watch the world of Fort de France pass by the wrought iron railings which protected the café from the street.

'I'm glad, now, that we've come too early for the Mardi Gras carnival,' said Mrs Ingram. 'Coming at this time, when it's quiet, we're able to look around and really see the place. I must say some of the women are remarkably attractive. That one at the next table, for instance. A very striking combination, don't you think, coffee-coloured skin contrasted with blonde hair?'

Of course they all turned to look and satisfy the curiosity she had aroused. Three people were sitting at the next table, two women and a man. The man was obviously French, neatly dressed, his hair cut *en brosse*. One of the women was brown-skinned and had fluffy black hair and wide dark eyes, but it was the other woman who commanded attention.

Tall and slim, fashionably dressed in a white trouser suit with a lime green shirt, she possessed a delicately-moulded profile, almost perfectly classical. Her complexion was pale brown and her long straight hair was blonde.

'She's like Josephine,' murmured Juanita, her brown eyes wide and startled. 'She could be Josephine. Don't you think so, Dawn?'

'Since Josephine was before my time, how can I tell?' replied Dawn tartly. She wasn't in a good mood, the result possibly of her roistering the previous day with Roger, or of an argument with Thomas. 'Her hair is dyed,' she commented, rather complacently, shaking back her own curling mane which was, rather surprisingly, naturally silvery blonde.

'Oh, do you mean Napoleon's Josephine?' asked Mrs Ingram, in all innocence.

'No. She means Roger's Josephine,' said Dawn out of the

108

corner of her mouth as she placed a cigarette between her lips.

'Who was she? A friend of his?' asked Mrs Ingram, still innocent.

'She was his *something*. Exactly what we'll never be quite sure, and you can bet your life Roger won't tell,' replied Dawn with a slightly bitter curve to her mouth. 'Probably the French would have a word for it. *Une liaison dangereuse*. Do you think that would fit, Nita? You know more than I do about that little affair, although I have it on good authority that Tom was involved too.'

Juanita looked worried and her glance flicked back from the tall elegant woman at the next table to her stepmother.

'Be careful what you say, Dawn,' she chided gently.

'Why should I be? It's no secret that the Gallant men have never been saints.' She laughed suddenly. 'Roger and I had a ball yesterday, even if I'm suffering slightly today as a result. The manager of the hotel agreed to let me sing in the cabaret with Danny accompanying me. I sang some of Roger's songs. The audience went wild. Danny thinks I could make a comeback.' Dawn's face was wistful as she tapped out ash on to an ash tray. 'I wish I could think he was right. It was great being in front of an audience again.'

'She's going,' said Juanita. She had been watching the woman in white and green. 'Oh, heavens! Roger is just coming in. Supposing it is Josephine and he sees her!'

'His reaction should be interesting,' remarked Dawn, sitting up and watching, her silvery grey eyes sharp as she glanced towards the entrance to the café. 'Especially since everyone says Josephine is dead.'

'It was never sure. She just disappeared,' said Juanita. They all watched the meeting. The woman smiled at Roger who had stood aside to allow her to pass through the doorway. She said something to him and he replied. When she had passed him he turned to watch her swing down the street with that graceful walk which all the women of Martinique seemed to possess.

'Well? Are we any the wiser?' asked Dawn drily.

'Not really. Roger is always so good at hiding his real feelings and he always looks after a pretty woman,' said Juanita with a sigh. 'Here come Ramon and Chuck with Father, thank goodness. Soon we can go for lunch. I could eat enough for two!'

They ate at a restaurant which specialised in local dishes. The tables were covered with checked tablecloths and the walls were covered with nostalgic murals of Parisian scenes, but the food was of Martinique—tiny pincushions of sea-urchins, which had been simmered in a marinade of bell peppers, garlic and lime juice, were served on a soup plate with crusty French bread. This delectable dish was followed by steak flamed in rum to which was added a fresh watercress salad.

When the meal was over there was some argument about the arrangements for the afternoon and soon Miranda found herself in a hired car with Mrs Ingram, Juanita and Chuck on her way to La Pagerie to see the birthplace of Napoleon's Josephine. She was not quite sure what had happened to Thomas and Dawn, but she hoped that they were together and that Dawn had not gone off with Roger again.

The actual homestead at La Pagerie had been ruined by a hurricane. However, there was a small museum containing mementoes of the childhood of the illustrious coquette. Miranda was not particularly impressed by the story of the woman whom she did not think had been especially pretty, who had been fourteen years older than Napoleon and had lied to him about her age.

Afterwards a drive around the southern part of the island gave glimpses of beauty which she would never forget. Shining white beaches festooned with fishing nets hung up to dry; little villages dozing quietly in the sun; lacework formed by giant tree ferns overhanging the road across the interior; and everywhere flowers, wild and cultivated. There were waxy anthuriums, their red heart-shaped discs glowing amongst huge heart-shaped leaves; gay and gaudy

110

hibiscus, its colours ranging from deep crimson to sun yellow; rich purple bougainvillaea cascading over walls; delicate fragrant frangipani and star-like spray orchids.

They returned to the yacht to pick up swimming suits and evening clothing before going across the bay to a hotel on the headland where they were to dine and dance. Only Mr Ingram was on board. Roger, Thomas and Dawn had not returned and when he realised that they had not gone on the tour of the island Mr Ingram was worried.

'I'd like a word with you, Miranda, before you go for that swim I know you're longing to take,' he said rather severely.

'Yes, Mr Ingram,' she replied dutifully. 'Is there any post for me yet?'

'I'm afraid not,' he replied. 'You did tell your aunt to send all her letters care of Mrs Phipps at head office, didn't you?'

'Yes, I did. I can't think why I haven't heard. I was sure there would be letters for me at Antigua.'

'Maybe there'll be something in Grenada. I'm hoping we'll be there the day after tomorrow. It's time some conclusion was reached regarding Fortuga. We can't go on cruising like this for ever. I'm being pushed by the company. Another island has come up for sale. The owner has tried to develop it on his own and has run out of capital. Head office says I've to let the Gallants stew in their own juice and go after this other place before Cosmopolitan Holdings get wind of it. The trouble is I hate to think I've been defeated by a young hedonist who hasn't a thought in his head beyond the sound of music and enjoying himself. There must be some way to make him accept our offer.'

'I don't think he will,' said Miranda. 'You see, he puts his sister first.'

Mr Ingram banged the desk with his fist. His eyes gleamed with triumph.

'His sister! She's the key,' he exclaimed. 'We must go to Fortuga and meet her. There's a chance she might see reason. Thomas has told me that she's a very clever woman and has astute business sense when it comes to money matters, which is more than can be said for her younger brother. Good. My thanks to you.'

'But I haven't done anything,' said Miranda uneasily.

'You mentioned Miss Gallant to me and that was enough to inspire me. Now off you go to the hotel, and remember to keep Chuck entertained. He's getting very impatient.'

To reach the hotel on the headland they had to cross the wide bay in a water taxi. They found Thomas sitting by the hotel's swimming pool with a party of Canadians from Montreal. He seemed happy enough with his new friends although slightly fuddled as if he'd had too many rum punches. He said he'd come to the hotel with Dawn and Roger but they had gone off somewhere, he wasn't quite sure where. Meantime he was having a ball and why didn't Zelda join him?

Primed by her husband to keep Thomas contented, Mrs Ingram consented with her always amiable smile and Miranda went with Chuck, Juanita and Ramon, first to swim in the pool and then to lie on the beach beneath coloured umbrellas.

'We've got to do something about Roger, Nita,' said Chuck as he flung himself down on the sand beside Miranda, who was lying prone, sifting the fine sand through her fingers. Juanita was sitting on the other side of Chuck, wringing water out of her long black tresses. She had tanned to an even teak colour and, in her hibiscus red sarong-type swimsuit, looked as if she had grown up on a tropical island beneath coconut palms beside the murmuring, glittering sea.

'I know,' agreed Juanita. 'He and Dawn are behaving abominably.'

'I've a feeling they're concocting something between them which Pop isn't going to like,' said Chuck.

'I have too. Dawn told us this morning that she sang at the place she and Roger visited in Antigua. She was thrilled to be in front of an audience again, and was talking of making a comeback.'

Chuck's laughter sounded scathing.

'She was never a star, so how can she make a comeback?' he jeered.

'She sings better now than she did, and she's more poised,' murmured Juanita seriously. 'With Roger's contacts in the musical world she could get back into the nightclub circuit, and then I doubt if anything could stop her. She has the right shape and looks for the sultry torch-singer style of singing.'

'And has learned to carry the torch for Roger,' jibed Chuck, 'unless of course he's now returning her interest in him. But I'm not really concerned about that. I'm concerned about this transaction with Transmarine. I've got to have that money. Pop's in debt up to the ears, and I'm not far behind him.'

'Oh, Chuck,' chided Juanita gently, 'how could you! I could ask Ramon for you, if you like.'

'I've asked him already and he coughed up like a good brother-in-law should,' said Chuck cynically. 'But I can't sponge on him any more, and Pop won't.'

'Which is something good to be said in his favour,' said Juanita.

'The only good thing. What a father! There must be some way of making Roger agree to sell. He doesn't live there and has no interest in developing the place. We need a weapon to use. Can't you think of anything, Nita? Something we could use to blackmail him with.'

'Now you're playing pirates,' accused Nita. 'We can't do anything until we get to Fortuga and can talk to Marnie. If she says she's willing to leave Gallant's Fancy, Roger hasn't any reason for keeping the place.'

'There's an idea,' drawled Chuck. 'If we can work on her and persuade her that she'll be doing us all a great favour by refusing to live there any longer, we have it made. Roger will do anything for her because he has a bad conscience where she's concerned. She makes him feel guilty because he feels responsible for her blindness. Have you any idea why?'

'No. But I know she's the only one who knows the truth about Josephine,' said Juanita. 'Did I tell you we saw someone very like her in the café this morning...'

Her voice was lowered to a confidential whisper and Miranda could hear no more. With a few words Juanita had brought vividly before her the woman in the café with her striking appearance, dark skin against blonde hair, the smile she had given Roger, his hesitation in the doorway of the café as he had looked after her. Had he also thought the woman had resembled Josephine? And what had Josephine, who had been Thomas's housekeeper, been to Roger? His *something*, Dawn had said scornfully, suggesting that there had been an affair between him and Josephine. According to Juanita only Marnie knew the truth.

Miranda sighed and buried her head on her arms. She wished she hadn't heard the conversation between brother and sister. Once again she was shocked at the way the Gallants schemed and plotted amongst themselves. Juanita and Chuck were no better than Thomas, their father, and now, like Mr Ingram, they hoped to persuade Marnie to join them as they ganged up against Roger. And he was no better than they, counter-plotting with Dawn, possibly using her in some way to hurt Thomas.

She wished there was someone she could talk to who wasn't involved in this struggle. She wished she was one of those cool efficient secretaries whom she admired. Her problem was that her feelings always got the better of her, reaching out to complete strangers, taking sides. She would be better off married to Joe. He was safe and sound.

Tears pricked her eyes suddenly. Would there be a letter waiting for her in Grenada? Had Joe missed her during the past two weeks? She tried to visualise him and couldn't. Aunt Clara and Dottie were also dim shapes in her mind. In fact it was hard to imagine that places like Dartford ex-

114

isted, whipped by the east wind which had blown in from the Thames estuary, when she was here basking on a beach under the caress of the sun.

'Come on, Miranda,' Chuck urged. 'One last swim before we change for dinner and then we're going to have the best night out we've had yet.'

Now that the sun was slipping down towards the rim of the sea, a perfect orange circle in a primrose-coloured sky streaked with feathery crimson clouds, his mood had changed. He was light-hearted, ready for any fun the long dark night might offer, buoyed up by the hope that all was not lost and there was still a way in which they could persuade the inflexible Roger to sell his portion of the Gallant estate.

She went swimming with him and then went with Juanita to the suite of rooms which the Ingrams had hired for the evening, to change into the simple evening dress which she had brought with her. It was pale turquoise in colour, high in the waist. The bodice was a simple cross-over making a deep V neckline at the back and the front. The skirt fell in stiff folds to the ground. The colour set off her tan and brought out the bluish light in her grey eyes. Somehow her hair did not look right with the simple Empire-style dress and Juanita, in a rush of friendliness, offered to arrange it for her, heaping it up on her head, lending her a silver chain to thread through the silken folds from which tiny little tendrils managed to escape to curl tantalisingly on her forehead and in front of her ears. When Miranda looked in the full-length mirror she hardly recognised the young woman who stood there so poised and elegant.

They went to the bar to join the others for a pre-dinner drink. Surprisingly Roger was there, distinguished in conventional black dinner suit which he wore with a magnificent ruffled shirt. He was talking to Mrs Ingram, but he looked up when Juanita and Miranda walked in. He grinned at Juanita and raised a hand in salute to her. His glance slid past Miranda, then came back to her as if he had not recognised her at first. He did not grin or wave his hand as he considered her appearance slowly, but a strange enigmatic expression passed over his face before he turned back to give Mrs Ingram all his polite attention again.

Of Dawn there was no sign and she did not join them for dinner. When Thomas asked Roger rather belligerently if he had seen her, Roger shrugged his shoulders and said he hadn't seen her since mid-afternoon. Seeing anger tauten Thomas's face Mr Ingram intervened diplomatically, put a brotherly arm around Thomas's shoulders and guided him into the dining room.

They dined with Thomas's Canadian friends. Miranda sat between Ramon and Chuck. On Chuck's left one of the tall Canadian girls sat and he seemed to have a great deal to discuss with her. The meal was a marvel of sophisticated simplicity. Tiny local clams seasoned with West Indian limes; heavenly lobster mayonnaise; veal cooked in a tantalising sauce. Champagne bubbled and a variety of liqueurs were served with the delicious coffee.

Afterwards they all went to the dance floor, which was out of doors, screened by white trellis, over which purple bougainvillaea tumbled, and illumined by hanging coloured lamps. Small tables and chairs were set round the edge of the floor, amongst which waiters moved deftly as they served drinks.

For a while they watched a group of local singers and dancers dressed in their national costumes as they performed the folk songs and dances of their island to the accompaniment of guitars and drums. Fascinated by the dances, which were a strange mixture of the sedate measures of the seventeenth and eighteenth century and the more abandoned rhythms and movements of African dances, Miranda sat by Mrs Ingram, oblivious to everything else until the group finished their programme. A small dance band appeared and began to play more familiar music for dancing. Several couples, including Chuck and the Canadian girl, and Ramon and Juanita, took the floor.

116

Mrs Ingram leaned back and spoke to someone who was sitting behind her in the shadow and glancing in that direction Miranda saw Roger sitting in the shadow of the trellis work. Coloured light glinted on the glass he raised to his lips and on the cuff-links of his shirt. She wondered how long he had been sitting there so quietly.

Resigning herself to sitting out for the evening because Chuck seemed more interested in the Canadian girl than herself, Miranda sipped a fruit punch brought to her by Ramon. Later she let him persuade her to dance a samba with him to a gay Caribbean calypso. The wind sighed through the palm trees and the smell of flowers was heady. In the black velvet of the sky, beyond the coloured lights, stars twinkled and she guessed that there were stars reflected in the sea, too.

She had hardly sat down when the band began to play another slower dance. She watched the couples who were dancing move close to each other, cheek to cheek. A hand touched her on the shoulder and she knew who was there by the tingle which crept along her nerves.

'Will you dance with me, Miranda, please?' Roger asked quietly.

She was afraid to dance with him to that slow seductive music, but she could scarcely refuse without seeming rude. Without looking at him she inclined her head and stood up. Still without looking she raised her hand to his shoulder. His arm slid round her waist, his other hand took hers and they moved off together.

She had intended to be withdrawn and stiff while she danced with him, keeping a cautious distance, but within seconds she was being held closely, her head against his shoulder, and it seemed right to be there. They danced effortlessly together as if made to be partners.

'What have you been doing today?' Roger asked softly.

'We went to Josephine's home,' she replied unthinkingly, and felt his arm go rigid under her fingers. She looked up and was surprised to see an expression of incredulity on his face. 'Oh, I mean we went to the birthplace of Napoleon's Josephine,' she aded hastily.

The disbelief on his face was replaced by an expression of amusement.

'She was a mendacious, scheming woman who managed to lead Napoleon a merrier chase than all the armies of Europe combined,' he remarked drily. But he was not quite casual enough. Miranda could tell that the name Josephine had disturbed him. 'Is that all you did?'

'We drove round the island. Now I understand why it's called the island of flowers.'

'*Madininia*, it was called by the original Carib and Arawak inhabitants, but the French have another name for it. They call it *l'Ile des Revenants*, the island one always returns to.'

'Have you been here often?' she asked.

'This is my second visit.'

Miranda rushed in blindly, wanting to know about *his* Josephine.

'The women here are different. They walk beautifully.'

'So you noticed? Native mothers have been known to carry their daughters' schoolbags so that the rhythm of the girls' walk shouldn't be spoiled. Josephine wasn't the only famous siren from Martinique, you know. Madame de Maintenon, wife of Louis the Fourteenth of France, came from here, as did the beautiful Aimée Dubuc de Rivery, mother of Sultan Mahmoud of the Berbers,' he replied.

'We saw a very striking woman in the café this morning,' persisted Miranda. 'She had dark skin and blonde hair. Nita said she was like someone she used to know, someone you used to know.'

'Nita talks too much. She always has,' he said coolly, and his hand tightened on hers. 'It's a bad habit some women have. Please don't fall into it, Miranda. I like you as you are, quiet and reserved. I saw the woman too. She wasn't like Josephine.'

The music came to an end. There was a roll of drums. A

118

man in evening dress stepped into the circle of light directed on to the middle of the floor by a powerful spotlight. He made an announcement in French, repeating it in English. He had a special guest singer that night, and hoped they would all enjoy her singing. He did not state the singer's name.

Music started up again, familiar, slightly atonal, not going exactly where one expected it to go, the music of *Stars in the Sea*. Roger guided Miranda across the floor away from Mrs Ingram, away from the platform on which the band were sitting, into a shadowy corner near some steps which led down to the garden of the hotel.

The spotlight came on again directed at the platform. It shone on a woman, tall and seductively curved, in a flattering gown which sparkled and winked, making the silver-gilt hair which hung past her shoulders in rippling, shimmering waves. She began to sing in a sultry, compelling voice; Dawn, dynamic and beautiful, singing the song which had brought fame to Roger.

Juanita and Chick had been right when they had guessed that Dawn and Roger had been plotting something between them which would annoy Thomas, thought Miranda, looking over in the direction of Thomas trying to see the expression on his face. But Roger swung her round and his body blocked her view as he turned and pulling her after him, hurried down the steps into the fragrant darkness of the garden. Along a path which twisted amongst poinsettias and oleanders he sped, light-footed, and, with her hand caught in his tight grasp, she could do nothing else but follow, her turquoise dress billowing out behind her.

There was a certain exhilaration in running through the dark warm night and her companion's mood soon communicated itself to her. She felt gay, light-hearted and, most unusual for Miranda, mischievous, and was not surprised when as they reached the beach, bone-white sand, luminous in the starlight beside the glinting black of the sea, Roger stopped running and turning to take both her hands in his, began to sing the words of Ariel's song from *The Tempest*, to a melody which she guessed he had composed himself.

'Come unto these yellow sands,
And then take hands,
Court'sied when you have, and kiss'd,
(The wild waves wist.)'

He stopped singing and pulled her towards him. Guessing his intention, Miranda pulled backwards in the opposite direction and demanded:

'Why have we come here?'

'In the first place, to escape Thomas's wrath at the sight of his wife singing,' he replied lightly.

'Coward!' she accused, and saw his teeth glimmer as he grinned unrepentantly.

'No. Only considerate of the feelings of others. I wouldn't have liked him to embarrass the Ingrams and the rest of the party by attacking me in public.'

'You encouraged Dawn to sing to torment him, didn't you?'

'I did it because she asked me,' he evaded smoothly. 'Who am I to refuse to do something for Dawn when she asks me and it's in my power to help her?'

'She asked you to use your influence so that she could sing here tonight as she sang last night in Antigua?' she exclaimed.

'She sings well, don't you think? It would be a pity for her talent to lie hidden for the rest of her life. During the past three years while it's been dormant it has matured. Now she can compete with the best and win,' he replied, still smooth.

'But your cousin will be angry, because to follow such a career she'll have to leave him,' protested Miranda.

Roger didn't reply and she realised he was still holding her hand, listening to the distant music of the band, his head tipped to one side. Miranda listened too.

'I like your music,' she offered shyly.

'Thank you,' he replied politely and rather vaguely.

'You must feel pleased that it's been so successful,' she tried again.

'Not particularly. That isn't the sort of music I ever wanted to compose. It just happened. It was written to please a very good friend of mine. Kit Williams.'

'I know.'

'You read the popular press?' His voice was cynical.

'Only recently,' she countered. 'What sort of music do you like to compose?'

'Perhaps I should have said I'd prefer to be remembered for something better than film music,' he replied, suddenly serious. 'At present I'm working on the music for a new ballet for John Mansfield, the choreographer. He's based it on Shakespeare's *The Tempest*. That's why I can quote the play by the yard and know all about Miranda.'

'It's Aunt Clara's favourite play. She quotes it by the yard too,' said Miranda with a laugh.

'Then you were called after that Miranda and not the other one,' he challenged.

'Yes, I'm afraid so,' she admitted.

The distant music had stopped and they could hear the sound of applause.

'She's made it,' murmured Roger, and there was a note of satisfaction in his voice. Miranda wondered with a strange feeling of envy if he were in love with Dawn and was trying to make her leave Thomas for good.

She tried to free her hands from his, but he tightened his hold.

'You haven't "court'sied" or kissed yet,' he murmured suggestively, pulling her towards him.

'I'm not going to,' she retorted, resisting that pull.

'Who's the coward now?' he taunted.

'You promised not to tease me any more,' Miranda argued, feeling her heart beginning to pound.

'Did I? But that was in the clear light of morning. Now it's the soft velvet darkness of the tropical night and here we are again on a sandy beach beneath tall palms, that most romantic of places. And although I sang Ariel's song, I'm no sprite, but a mere mortal, male in gender, who can't stand to be near you any longer without kissing you.'

A sharp jerk and she was in his arms. Sensing the difference in him compared with that other night, she lifted her head. All her resolves to have nothing to do with him melted and she was ready for his kiss which this time came not as a threat but as the expression of a heartfelt desire to kiss her. She returned it in full measure, a little shyly, trying out her new knowledge learned recently from him, so that when he stopped kissing her, he said huskily:

'That's better. You're learning, and why not? This is Martinique, the island of love as well as flowers, where people live for the sheer pleasure of loving. Why shouldn't we also take what the present offers and have something to remember when we grow old?'

His lips found hers again and Miranda didn't resist. Then they walked beside the softly glimmering murmuring sea, holding hands, not speaking because they had no need of speech, both of them caught in a magic spell woven around them by the island; a spell woven of sea music and flower scents, starlight and glittering sand, black velvet shadow and whispering palms.

Miranda had no idea how far they walked. She seemed to float over the ground tirelessly like a spirit. She could have walked all night as long as Roger was with her, holding her hand.

They turned at last. He said something about having to go back to the hotel and the spell was broken. Their minds went off in different directions, hers leaping in thought to Thomas, then to Dawn, and from Dawn to the woman in the white suit and lime-coloured shirt she had seen in the café that morning, who had resembled another woman called Josephine.

'Who was Josephine?' she asked.

'Must you know?' Roger countered warily.

'Do you object to *me* knowing?' she replied gently.

'As long as you don't use your knowledge against me,' he parried.

'I would never do that,' she said gravely.

He swung her round so that they were face to face again, the sheen of eyes and skin showing faintly in the starlight.

'I believe you mean that, but of course, you're Miranda and you mean everything you say,' he mocked. 'I wonder if you mean everything you do?'

Before she could answer he urged her forward along the beach towards the glittering hotel.

'Josephine was Thomas's housekeeper for a while, at Gallant's Folly,' he said quickly. 'She was Martiniquaise, beautiful, seductive, like the woman you saw today.'

'What happened to her?'

'She ran away.'

'Why?'

Roger didn't answer. They had reached the steps going up to the dance floor. He released her hand. She caught his arm, sensing that he was going to leave her there.

'Why, Roger?'

'I ... I can't tell you why,' he said gruffly, then bent his head, kissed her, a hard forceful kiss of farewell. 'Good night, Miranda,' he said in a curiously shaken voice. 'Our ways part here.'

Then he was gone, walking swiftly away into the shadows, and she was alone.

CHAPTER FIVE

KEEPING to her resolve to see every departure and arrival whenever it was possible, Miranda was up early again the next morning to watch *Sea Quest* slip out of the harbour, as rose-tinted clouds fanned out behind the island of flowers.

Leaning alone on the rail at the stern, she watched the Diamond Rock at the southernmost tip of Martinique fade slowly into the shimmering distance. Her thoughts at seeing the island to which she would never return dip below the horizon were too deep for expression and so she looked as always, quiet and composed, slim and slight in checked cotton pants and blue cotton shirt, her sun-kissed hair blown back from her face, revealing the fragile line of bone from shoulder to jaw and the small rounded ears. Apart from the golden tan she could be taken as the same girl who had left the plane at San Juan airport over two weeks ago. Only she knew that inwardly she would never be the same again.

She turned her back on Martinique and all that had happened there. When Roger had said that their ways had parted at the bottom of the steps in the hotel garden the previous night she sensed that he had meant more than he had said. He had meant that there would be no more walks beside the sea in the dark, no more lingering together in the early morning watching islands come up out of the sea. All that was over and finished; a brief melody, a few bars of music which the composer has cast aside, never to be used again; a dream, to be remembered perhaps occasionally, but never to be fully realised.

Walking along the side-deck to the bow she noticed new islands looming misty blue, beckoning the traveller to partake of their special delights. Miranda felt her heart lift at the sight of them as she listened to the steady throb of powerful engines and heard the rushing sound of water as the yacht thrust aside the rolling waves of the blue sea in its hurry to go south. Soon she would be in St Georges, Grenada, where there would be a letter from Joe waiting for her.

No one came to join her that morning on the sun-deck and there was no one having breakfast in the main saloon. Only Billy the West Indian steward was there, excited and talkative because they were going to Grenada where he had been born and where he would see his family.

'Yes, ma'am, it's one honey of an island,' he drawled. 'Just you wait until you smell those spices, you aren't ever going to forget them.'

'Do only spices grow there?' asked Miranda, thinking that if all the natives of Grenada were as jolly and gentle as Billy was she would enjoy her brief stay there.

'Bananas, sugar apples, children and good cricketers grow there too,' replied Billy with his wide grin, placing fruit juice in front of her. He glanced across the saloon, his attention caught by a movement. 'Good morning, Mrs Gallant,' he chanted. 'What would you like this morning? There's a fresh pineapple juice, I squeezed it myself, and fresh bananas with cereal and cream.'

Dawn approached the table with her swaying seductive walk. She was dressed in a shocking pink, be-ruffled, almost sheer negligée and her silvery hair streamed over her shoulders. She looked cool, beautiful and very, very hard.

'Coffee, please. Black and plenty of it. Nothing else,' she said, with a smile which made Billy roll his eyes appreciatively before he went off to the galley, singing a calypso which he had made up himself and which was all about the good ship *Sea Quest* and the people who sailed in her.

Dawn sat down opposite to Miranda, her silvery glance flicking over Miranda's gold-bloomed cheeks and shining sun-kissed hair.

'No Gallant to share your morning with today?' she asked insolently.

125

Miranda glanced up warily and decided not to rise to the bait.

'You sang wonderfully last night,' she said.

A quick frown twitched Dawn's finely-plucked eyebrows together.

'Sounds to me as if you've been taking lessons on how to change the subject,' she remarked tartly. 'How long were you on the beach with Roger last night? Obviously long enough to pick up a few hints from him. If you liked the way I sang why didn't you stay to hear me? I suppose you saw a chance of getting him to yourself for an hour. You won't be able to hold him, you know, he's like quicksilver. No woman I ever heard of could hold Roger.'

'Not even you?' asked Miranda, and shivered a little as the silvery eyes sent her a dagger-sharp glance.

'I could have had him at one time, but only on his terms. He's only interested in brief relationships with women, and at the time I, like the little romantic fool I was then, longed for something permanent and secure. Thomas seemed to offer that, so I accepted his proposal and learned the hard way why it's always been considered more satisfactory to be a Gallant's Fancy rather than a Gallant's Folly.'

Dawn made a little grimace of distaste at her own choice of words and reached for a cigarette from the packet she had brought to the table.

'I've no wish to hold anyone,' replied Miranda coolly, 'least of all Roger Gallant. He's not the sort of man who attracts me. Besides, I'm going to be married when I return to England.'

Dawn's eyes widened as she exhaled smoke from the freshly-lit cigarette.

'Oh? That's interesting. Does Roger know?'

'Yes.'

Dawn's eyes narrowed, grew speculative and then she nodded slowly.

'I can see now why you've caught his fancy for a while. You're different from the usual run of women he meets, the recording artists and the film starlets. That self-contained manner creates an impression of mystery which would tantalise a person of his enquiring mischievous temperament. He'd be wanting to find out the truth about you, to see if there's really any depth to such still waters. He'd be disappointed when he found that there was no mystery after all, only a little Girl Friday dreaming of the day she would be married to her nice dull suburban boy-friend. Poor Roger! It wouldn't be the first time he's had his illusions about a woman shattered, but his disillusionment makes him an interesting if sometimes cruel lover.'

'Is he your lover?' Miranda could not help asking the question which sprang out of a new agonising pain which seemed to be tearing her apart.

'Not yet, but he will be when he's come to terms with Thomas,' drawled Dawn, smiling faintly.

Billy had come with her coffee and there was no chance of more conversation. Not that Miranda wished to continue a conversation which was becoming more and more distasteful to her. With a muttered excuse she left the table while Billy was still pouring the coffee.

Fortunately Miranda was kept fairly busy for the rest of the day. After one of his discussions with Thomas and Roger, Mr Ingram called her to his office to type out some letters which he wished to have ready to post in Grenada. She thought he looked rather worried and tired, unlike the smooth executive whose real estate deals were the talk of head office. Was it possible he was growing tired of the cruise? Was the effort of keeping on good terms with the various very different members of the Gallant family getting on his nerves?

When she had finished the letters she gave them to him to sign, then slipped them into their envelopes and prepared to leave. It was almost four o'clock and she wanted to have a look at the islands through which they were passing before the sun set.

'Is that all, Mr Ingram?' she asked.

He came out of deep thought which was not pleasing him much judging by the cleft between his eyebrows.

'Hmm? Oh—er, yes. Please sit down, Miranda.' She sat on the edge of a chair and hoped he would not be long. 'You weren't present when that unpleasant little scene between Thomas and his wife took place at the hotel last night, were you?'

'No. I went for a walk.'

'Ah, yes. So did Roger Gallant. It was clever of him to disappear just at an awkward moment. He's an elusive character, even more so than Thomas, who was extremely upset when his wife appeared on the stage. Apparently when they married she promised to give up her career as a night-club singer.'

'She has a lovely voice,' murmured Miranda.

'That's as may be,' returned Mr Ingram testily. 'But that little performance was no help to me at all. Thomas actually accused me in front of everyone who was there of deliberately throwing Dawn and Roger together. It was most embarrassing.'

Miranda looked down at her hands. She did so in order to hide a smile. For wasn't that exactly what Mr Ingram had done? He had encouraged Dawn to seek out Roger and his scheme had boomeranged on him, causing him more trouble than he had anticipated.

'She's not been able to achieve anything,' he was grumbling about Dawn. 'I can't pin Roger down to any agreement at all. I wish now that we could bypass Grenada and go straight to Fortuga to see Miss Gallant before he causes any more trouble between Thomas and his wife, and before Thomas starts playing any of his tricks. He's talking of selling to another company. But we have to call at St Georges to collect mail, so we may as well show them the hotel there. I only hope you can keep Chuck happy.' He gave her a searching glance. 'So far you haven't been much help at all and I've a funny suspicion that you've let your feelings interfere.'

128

Miranda left the office feeling a little apprehensive. There was no doubt that this time the pleasant relaxed atmosphere had been shattered. Thomas had kept to his cabin all day. Chuck was sulky and silent, spending his time in the bar drinking rum punches. Juanita and Ramon had also kept out of sight, although Ramon did appear at dinner to inform the Ingrams that his wife wasn't feeling well and that he intended to take her to San Juan as soon as they could get a flight out of Grenada.

Only Dawn and Roger seemed to be unaffected by the previous night's events, lying about on the sun-deck, talking in whispers and often laughing.

'She's quite shameless,' complained Mrs Ingram of Dawn. 'But then people connected with the entertainment world often are.'

Sea Quest rushed on through the dark tropical night, its propeller churning up phosphorescence in the water, creating stars in the sea. Miranda lingered for a while at the railing of the sun deck, but on hearing voices behind her and recognising them as belonging to Dawn and Roger murmuring together in the intimate darkness, she left the lovely warm night to them, trying to ignore the sharp twist of jealousy she felt and wondering why the knowledge that Roger preferred Dawn's company to her own should hurt so much.

In her cabin she prepared for bed, then lay on her bunk listening to the sound of the water pushing against the hull of the yacht. Tomorrow when she awoke the yacht would be in harbour. Surely there would be letters waiting for her from Aunt Clara and Joe. She would take the morning off and go and visit Mrs Mowat's friend Laura Bolton. They would talk about England and familiar things and she would find relief for a few hours from the complications of Mr Ingram's wheeling and dealing, from the plotting of the Gallants, and above all from the strange pain she was feeling at the thought that Roger had lost interest in her.

Lulled by the roll of the yacht, she slept. When she

awoke the rolling had stopped. Looking through the porthole, she saw the roofs of sturdy buildings covered with red pantiles glowing in the sunshine, clustering round the harbour of smooth blue water.

Dressing quickly in shorts and shirt, she went up on deck to look at St Georges, a town of solidly built buildings climbing up a hillside amongst vivid tropical plants and bushes. Behind the hill towered another higher hill with a dead crater at its summit.

On the mirror-like water of the harbour an old trading schooner, some of its sails set, was inching forward to the entrance. Small rowing boats manned by skinny brown boys were setting out from the wharfs to meet the big cruise ship which was approaching cautiously to anchor nearby, being too big to tie up to any of the wharfs.

By the time Miranda was ready to leave the yacht, after having made arrangements to meet the Ingrams at the hotel in the afternoon, the sun was high and hot, beating down on the stone quayside. Wearing the sun-dress she had bought in St Thomas as well as the white sun-hat given to her by Roger, she walked towards the entrance to the wharfs. Beyond the gates she could see a crowd of Grenadians waiting for the tourists coming off the cruise ship, and soon she was amongst them as they swarmed round her and in their lilting voices told her their names and offered to drive her anywhere on the island.

Miranda laughed, not knowing which of the smiling cheerful young men to choose, and they laughed with her. In the end she chose one called Elvin who looked poorer and younger than any of the others. When she saw his car she wondered if she had chosen well, because the old Morris looked as if it was about to disintegrate and it wouldn't start until it had been coaxed and finally kicked.

They set off slowly in the direction of the town centre, but once the engine had warmed up they were soon weaving in and out of the traffic and careering round the bends of the switchback streets, dodging the gaily painted buses on

130

the way.

The boutique which Laura Bolton owned was on Granby Street, and Elvin waited outside while Miranda went into the shop to make sure Laura was there.

The Cave, as the boutique was called, sold imports from England as well as some of Laura's own pottery and pictures and the creations of other local artists and craftsmen. Laura was a graceful young woman of about twenty-seven with braided blonde hair and cornflower blue eyes, and was delighted to see someone from England. Handing over the care of the boutique to her assistant, she decided to take Miranda to her home for lunch and together they sat in the back seat of Elvin's taxi-cab as it rattled through the town again and out along the road which wound round the harbour to the marina. On the way they passed wooden houses, their verandahs overhung with the inevitable bougainvillaea, in front of which turbanned brown-skinned women stood and gossiped. A group of schoolgirls in tunics and blouses ran home from school for their lunch. On a playing field almost bare of grass which was near a factory, two teams of men were playing cricket.

A sharp right turn and they reached the yacht marina where all sorts and sizes of sailing yachts were tied up to floating docks. Nearby were several new bungalows. Laura asked Elvin to stop in front of the one at the end of the street which had a view of the sea.

Arrangements were made for Elvin to come back and pick Miranda up to take her to the hotel and the two women went into the pretty wooden bungalow. Laura explained that her husband Keith was away skippering a big cruising yawl for some Americans who had chartered it for a holiday.

In the small well-equipped kitchen they made lunch together, chattering all the time, exchanging information about each other. Miranda learned all about the Boltons' voyage across the Atlantic three years previously, of how they loved the way of life on the island and had managed to find themselves work there. Laura on the other hand learned all about Miranda's cruise through the islands and her visits to various well-known attractions.

'You've had a simply fabulous trip,' commented Laura. 'And I'm interested in your news about the Gallants. I can't believe that they'll sell.'

'Do you know any of them?'

'Not personally, but I've heard about them. Everyone here knows and takes pride in Kit Williams' success as a singer, and of course it's impossible to mention him without the story being told about the song which made him famous and which Roger Gallant composed. Then Keith always makes Fortuga one of his ports of call when he takes a party on a cruise. He says the little marina there is one of the best in the Caribbean. He knows Aubrey Vincent who manages the estate for Marnie Gallant. Apparently the island is fast becoming one of the more popular "get-away-from-it-all" kind of resort, where you can be alone with nature and yet have all mod cons handy at the same time. Marnie is a whizz at knowing how to develop the potentialities of the place.'

'How has she done it? I thought she was blind?'

'She is, but she has a feeling for the land. She's planted all sorts of fruit trees and is now marketing fruit as well as sugarcane. Aubrey does the work, but she has the ideas. Keith says theirs is a great partnership and they're in love with each other, but Aubrey won't ask her to marry him.'

'Why not?'

'I don't know. You might find out when you go there. If you do please write and tell me.'

'Has Keith met either Thomas or Roger?' asked Miranda.

'He hasn't met Thomas. He left the island several years ago and his half of the estate is in a deplorable state. As for Roger,' Laura paused and wrinkled her forehead as she tried to recall her husband's comments, 'Keith met him once. He was there on one of his short visits to see his sister.

Keith said he seemed friendly enough on the surface, but difficult to know, and that under the friendly show there was a deep reserve, as if Roger didn't want people to know the real Roger Gallant.'

Miranda nodded in agreement and they talked of other subjects while they ate lunch on the screened-in verandah with its views of the sea. The time passed quickly and Miranda left just after two o'clock to take another crazy ride with Elvin, along a narrow twisting road. He honked his horn before every bend to make sure there were no stray children in his way and slowed down for the wide culverts which crossed the road and which were necessary, he explained, to carry the water away during the heavy rains.

Eventually the wild lush vegetation of banana and coconut palms gave way to cultivated fields. They turned off the road to drive along another newly made road between rows of tall palms. This took them to a courtyard screened from the road by hibiscus, poinsettia and other exotic shrubs, all ablaze with colour.

After paying Elvin and thanking him for his help, Miranda entered the hotel and walked down a cool, stone-floored corridor which flanked a patio where a fountain played into an oblong pool. There she found the reception desk and was informed by the pleasantly-smiling Grenadian woman where she could find Mrs Ingram.

The end of the stone-floored corridor opened directly on to the area around the swimming pool which was close to the beach. Lounging under gaily striped umbrellas were Thomas and Mrs Ingram with a group of Americans with whom Thomas had struck up one of his sudden and hearty friendships.

'How glad I am to see you,' said Mrs Ingram in a low voice to Miranda. 'We're having a terrible day. I wish you hadn't gone to see your friend. We needed you here. Roger and Dawn have disappeared again and Doug is having a meeting with someone who owns an island in the Grenadines which he would like to sell to Transmarine. Juanita

133

and Ramon have flown back to San Juan. Such a pity. She wasn't feeling very well and he thought it would be safer if she were at home and near her own doctor.'

'Where's Chuck?' asked Miranda, searching the pool and then the apron to see if he was amongst the swimming crowd.

'He's gone down to the beach. Please go and find him. I'm afraid he'll go off too and then we'll be left with this awful Thomas on our hands.'

The beach was the most beautiful Miranda had ever seen. It stretched for miles, curving beside limpid green water. She found Chuck sitting beneath one of the high palm trees bargaining with a group of pedlars who were trying to sell him Barbadian cotton shirts, palm leaf hats, baskets of spice, coconuts and fruit.

He saw Miranda approach and greeted her with a wide grin.

'I'm doing my best to beat her down,' he said, pointing to a very thin elderly Grenadian woman who was wearing a cotton turban swathed around her head and a long dress with a full skirt. She greeted Miranda with a smile and introduced herself as Virginia and immediately spread out a long-skirted, halter-topped sun-dress made from purple cotton decorated with African-style patterns in many different colours.

'Missy buy dress,' she urged.

In no time Virginia's daughter, who was called Isobel, and her little boy Philip, arrived to persuade Chuck and Miranda to buy spices and fruit. Then came a young man called William, who was Virginia's youngest son, and offered to weave a hat from broad green palm leaves there and then before their eyes. Behind him came Virginia's husband, a short squat man with a seamed brown face and a flat nose. He held out a coconut and produced a wicked-looking knife called a *machete*. When Miranda agreed to buy the coconut for a few cents, he lopped the top off it with the knife and handed it to her so that she could drink the milk from it. When she had done that he carefully cut the coconut up into small pieces so that she and Chuck could eat it.

There was much joking and laughter while the bargaining went on and when at last the pedlars moved on to another part of the beach, Miranda and Chuck surveyed their bargains with a certain amount of rueful amusement.

'Both of us are several dollars lighter after that,' sighed Chuck. 'I only hope the guys back in Washington are going to appreciate me in this shirt.' He held the loose, brightly-coloured gaily-patterned, slit-necked shirt he had bought against him and perched the palm-leaf hat on his head. 'Have you thought of what you're going to do in London with that sun-dress you've bought?'

'I shall wear it about the house, and when I do I'll think of you in Washington wearing your shirt,' she replied gaily.

'Will you?' His eyes darkened and he seemed pleased at the thought as he put a friendly arm around her. 'That's nice of you, Miranda. But then you're a nice girl. Far too nice to be mixed up with a gang of pirates like us. I'm glad you've come down to the beach. I was feeling pretty blue and in need of diversion. If I'd had enough money I'd have flown back to the States from here. I've had enough of Ingram's cruise. It hasn't got us anywhere with Roger. Why doesn't Ingram admit that he's lost out on this deal, and give Pop and me a chance to do business with some other combine who wouldn't be interested in the Fancy?'

Miranda didn't answer his question which she hoped was rhetorical and didn't require an answer. Instead, afraid that he might get amorous again, she suggested that they swam, and he agreed.

After floating and swimming in the calm buoyant water, they returned to the hotel to join the Ingrams and Thomas. From there they went straight to the *Sea Quest* because Mr Ingram was keen to leave for Fortuga immediately.

At the harbour there was a slight delay because neither Dawn nor Roger seemed to be on board and, quite naturally, Thomas refused to leave until his wife turned up. Both he and Doug Ingram were showing signs of strain when Chuck spotted Roger strolling along the careenage where the yachts were tied up. He was with a pretty brown-skinned woman and there was no sign of Dawn.

'Roger!' Thomas's shout was stentorian and his cousin heard and turned his head to glance in the direction of the yacht. He waved his hand, but made no attempt to come towards them or to leave his companion.

'Dammit! What's he done with Dawn?' growled Thomas. 'I suggest, Ingram, that you ask one of the crew to go and fetch him. We'll be here all night if you don't.'

Doug Ingram did as he had been asked and eventually Roger came strolling with leisurely grace up the gangway.

'Where's Dawn?' demanded Thomas belligerently.

'I've really no idea,' drawled Roger. 'She said she might come back to the yacht, when I last saw her. Have you looked in your cabin?'

He was cool and unperturbed as he stood gazing at his cousin through the baffling blankness of his sun-glasses, and Thomas looked a little taken aback. Muttering that he hadn't thought of looking for Dawn in their cabin, he stumped off down the companionway to the lower deck, and Roger turned to lean on the railing of the sun-deck between Mr Ingram and Miranda.

'I'd like to get to Fortuga as soon as possible,' said Mr Ingram, with a touch of irritation.

'The sooner the better as far as I'm concerned,' replied Roger coldly. 'Why not give the order to cast off now? If you do we'll be there soon after sundown.'

He strolled away and after a few minutes Mr Ingram went along to the wheelhouse to give orders to leave.

Miranda wandered down to her cabin reflecting rather dismally that Mr Ingram had said nothing about any letters for her. While she was having a shower she felt the yacht lurch as it left the quayside, and by the time she had dried herself she could tell by the slightly rolling motion that it

136

had left the harbour and was on the open sea, on its way to Fortuga at last.

Fortuga. That meant seeing Gallant's Fancy and meeting Marnie Gallant, who according to Laura Bolton was a wizard at making the most of the island where she lived. If that were the case would Marnie be influenced so easily by Mr Ingram and Thomas Gallant and be willing to agree to the sale of Gallant's Fancy?

Miranda frowned as she slipped into a simple sleeveless cotton dress. She was half tempted to tell Roger that pressure was going to be put on his sister, but to do so would mean seeking him out deliberately, and that was something she did not want to do, partly because it would betray to him a little how she felt about him and partly because he had ignored her completely ever since the night they had walked together on the starlit beach in Martinique.

Our ways part here, Miranda, he had said, and he had meant it in two ways, she was convinced. As Dawn had implied yesterday morning, for a while Roger's fancy had been caught by a shy, quiet girl who didn't talk much, and he'd wanted to find out more about her. When he'd discovered that there wasn't very much to find out, he'd lost interest.

Miranda frowned again, not liking her thoughts, and the conch shell winked back at her, twinkling with pink light. Supposing he had lost interest, it didn't matter. She hadn't expected anything from him, so why be hurt when he turned away? Kissing and holding hands with a woman meant nothing to him, so why should she let it mean anything to her?

She sat down suddenly on the bed, her head in her hands, swaying back and forth, struggling with a tempest of desire which swept through her, a storm of feeling which was new to her and over which she seemed to have no control. Her body burned with longing to be with Roger, to walk with him under the stars, to kiss him and to be kissed by him, to make love with him.

137

A sharp knock on the cabin door startled her. She stiffened and caught sight of herself in the mirror. Her cheeks were scarlet and her eyes glittered strangely.

The knock was repeated.

'Miranda, are you there? It's me, Zelda. May I come in?'

Miranda sprang off the bed and opened the door. Mrs Ingram, who was wearing one of her excellently cut long dresses, looked agitated and a red flush stained her cheeks and neck too.

She did not seem to notice Miranda's agitation, but came right into the cabin and sat down on one of the beds.

'Mrs Gallant has gone,' she announced breathlessly. 'She wasn't in her cabin after all.'

'Gone where?'

'That's the trouble. She didn't say in the note she left for Thomas. She just wrote that she wouldn't be coming to Fortuga with us. Thomas is almost bursting blood vessels. He wanted Doug to turn back to Grenada at once. He said that Doug had no right to leave the harbour before he'd found out for sure whether Dawn was on board or not. He's right, of course.'

Miranda sat down too, shock making her legs suddenly weak as she remembered Roger smoothly suggesting that Dawn was in her cabin and then, just as smoothly, suggesting that if Mr Ingram wished to reach Fortuga soon after sundown he should give orders to cast off the yacht immediately.

'Then,' continued Mrs Ingram, having caught her second breath, 'Thomas turned on Roger and accused him of knowing Dawn's whereabouts.'

'What did Roger say to that?'

'He smiled in that tantalising way of his and said that he knew, but would only tell on certain conditions once we've reached Fortuga.'

Miranda recalled Dawn talking complacently about Roger coming to terms with Thomas. Had the time arrived

138

for the striking of a bargain between the two cousins, a bargain which involved Dawn? Her hands clenched in her lap as she tried to control the violent revulsion of feeling she was experiencing as she realised that Roger was just as much a pirate at heart as his older cousin. How could she have longed to be with him so passionately scarcely five minutes ago?

'What happened then?' she asked huskily.

'There was an awful scene. Thomas went nearly berserk. He called Roger a blackmailer and several other unpleasant names. It would have been better if Roger had retaliated, but he merely sat there and looked at Thomas as if he were some strange phenomenon. Then Chuck intervened and suggested to his father that they ought to hear what Roger had in mind, and all three of them went off to Roger's cabin. I hope they stay there until we reach Fortuga. I've had quite enough of them all, and I'll be glad when this cruise is over. Doug and I have often had to entertain peculiar people in the interests of business, but we've never come across anyone as difficult as Thomas Gallant or as vague and elusive as Roger Gallant.'

Mrs Ingram sighed wearily, and Miranda, soft-hearted as she was, felt a pang of sympathy for her.

'You won't repeat a word of any of this when we reach head office, will you, Miranda?' said Mrs Ingram suddenly, leaning forward urgently. 'It will be such a blow to Doug's self-esteem if he doesn't pull off the deal. He has pinned his hopes on Miss Gallant, but if she's anything like her brother we may as well give up hoping now.'

As Roger had predicted *Sea Quest* sidled into the small harbour on Fortuga island as the sun slipped below the horizon, leaving the sky streaked with rose and lemon light. Miranda's first impression of the island was of low-lying hills covered with lush vegetation silhouetted against the sky, backing a small village of white-painted wooden houses, encircling a placid almost land-locked harbour.

The yacht sidled up to a wharf, warps were thrown

ashore to smiling dark-skinned boys who made them fast. A broad-shouldered man in white, his coffee-coloured face split in two by a wide beaming smile, came down the gangway to shake hands with Roger who had appeared from his cabin just as the yacht had approached the wharf. He introduced the man in white to the Ingrams as Sam Williams, the elder brother of Kit the singer, and then announced smoothly that he and his cousins would spend the night ashore at Gallant's Fancy. Next morning he would send a car to pick up the Ingrams and Miranda to take them out to the house which was the other side of the island.

Coolly polite, completely in charge of the situation, very much the landowner on his own ground, he shook hands with the Ingrams, thanked them for their hospitality aboard the *Sea Quest* and then shepherded a rather subdued Thomas and Chuck ashore. There was no word from any of them for Miranda, only a backward glance and a wave of his hand from Chuck before all three of them disappeared into the darkness beyond the bright lights of the wharf.

The night passed quietly on board the yacht and next morning Miranda slept late for once. In fact she had only just dressed when Mrs Ingram came to tell her that the car from Gallant's Fancy had arrived to take them to the house where they were to have lunch with Marnie Gallant. Quickly she changed her clothing, deciding to wear her bikini beneath a blue cotton gingham skirt and blouse in case there was any chance of swimming or sunbathing after the meal.

The car was driven by a smiling young man who introduced himself, in the friendly island way, as James Williams, a cousin of Kit, and as he drove them through the village and across the island he took pride in pointing out the small new airport, built entirely by islanders, the well-tended fields of vegetables, the old distillery where the Gallants had first made rum in the seventeenth century, the groves of fruit trees which were a new and successful enterprise started by Marnie Gallant a few years previously and now beginning to show results.

They approached the house along a narrow winding drive up the side of a hill and came upon it suddenly as the drive widened into a pleasant courtyard paved with stone where two fountains played and hibiscus, allamanda and crepe myrtle bushes flaunted their blooms, towered over by that flame of the forest, the tulip tree.

The house was a surprise. Built of English red brick brought over by an earlier Gallant, it was classical in design, gracious and well-proportioned, typical of the English colonial period with its portico supported on graceful white pillars. A flight of wide white steps led up to the doorway and at the top of the steps stood three people waiting to greet the visitors.

One of them was Marnie Gallant, who resembled her brother only in so far that she possessed the same symmetry of facial features. Her hair was fair and streaked with grey. She wore it in a roughly cropped urchin style which drew attention to the fine line of jaw and nose. Her eyes were hidden by sun-glasses and she was dressed casually in white cotton slacks and a red and white striped T-shirt, both of which emphasised her slim boyish figure. Like Roger, on first meeting, she did not look her age, and it was difficult to believe she was over thirty-five.

Behind her stood Roger. He was in belted white pants and a dark blue shirt, casually elegant as always, making everyone else seem untidy and over-dressed. Beside him another man, tall and broad-shouldered with a dark-hued face and crinkly black hair, who had the clearest grey eyes Miranda had ever seen, stood silently, his powerful forearms, revealed by the rolled-up sleeves of his white shirt, crossed on his chest; an impressive giant of a man. He was introduced by Roger as Aubrey Vincent, the manager of the estate. There was no sign of Thomas or Chuck.

As she went forward rather shyly to shake hands with Marnie, Miranda found her hand gripped by both of the other woman's hands. Marnie's smile was warm and candid, as open as the day.

'So you are Miranda, "peerless, perfect Miranda", as Shakespeare put it,' she murmured in a soft voice which had more of a West Indian lilt to it than Roger's had. 'You won't mind if I touch your face, I hope? I learn so much about a person if I can feel her features, and I'm sure you're sizing me up and thinking what an untidy, ramshackle sister Roger has. I've never been able to compete with him in elegance.' Marnie's chuckle was infectious. 'I take after my mother, who was small and fair. Roger is a throwback to some red-headed rogue of a pirate. I expect you've had a taste already of his freebooting ways. He pretends he's much too civilised to be a pirate, but I know better.'

Marnie chuckled again and Miranda joined in her laughter, aware that Roger had discreetly guided the Ingrams and Aubrey into the house so that she and his sister could be alone for a few minutes.

Long-fingered hands trailed over her lips and cheeks, lingered around her eyes and finally slipped over her smooth hair.

'Lovely hair, Miranda, soft and silky as hair should be. Firm peach-like cheeks. But your mouth is too sensitive and you've been hurt recently. Not bad news from home, I hope?' asked Marnie.

A little alarmed by Marnie's perspicacity, Miranda stiffened slightly and her thoughts flew to the letter in her handbag. Mr Ingram had handed it to her just before they had left the yacht, having discovered it amongst the mail he had collected in Grenada the previous day. She had read it quickly in the car coming across the island. It had been from Aunt Clara and it had contained one item of astonishing news which she had not yet absorbed properly.

But how could this blind woman with the compassionate mouth possibly know that the news had not been good?

'I'm sorry, Miranda,' said Marnie, sensing her withdrawal. 'Keep it to yourself for now. Later when we know each other better, and Roger has promised there'll be time

142

for me to know you, you might like to tell me what's hurt you. What colour are your eyes? Colour is something I can't feel and is something I miss in my life.'

'They're bluish-grey, like those of most English girls, and my hair is dark brown. I'm really very ordinary,' replied Miranda.

Marnie nodded to herself.

'I can see you now, but you aren't ordinary. You're different. You're quiet and gentle, and you keep your thoughts and feelings to yourself too much. A young woman whose name can bring a strange note of awe to the voice of my rogue of a brother can't possibly be ordinary. But I'm neglecting my duties as a hostess. Give me your arm and we'll go together through the house to the patio where we'll have lunch.'

To Miranda's surprise the back of the house was entirely Spanish in design and quite old. Built of local stone which had been painted white, it had the high windows and tiny wrought iron balconies she had noticed on the houses in San Juan and its massive door opened on to a cool shaded patio which overlooked the sea.

Lunch was served informally as a buffet laid out on a long table from which they helped themselves to cold meats, crayfish salad and fruit salads. The conversation was kept deliberately light by Marnie, who seemed adept at soothing any ruffled feelings from which Doug Ingram might be suffering. In fact Miranda found it amusing to see both Ingrams succumbing to the kind of treatment they had given Thomas and Roger during the cruise.

She also watched Aubrey Vincent. There was no doubt about his affection for Marnie. He anticipated her every need and the expression in his clear eyes often gave him away. On the other hand Marnie had a way of teasing him gently which showed how she felt about him. Obviously they were in love with each other, yet something was keeping them apart. Was the barrier Marnie's blindness?

Miranda's glance strayed in Roger's direction and immediately her nerves leapt in tingling reaction, for he was watching her with amusement glinting in his eyes as if he guessed at her thoughts.

When the meal was over the soothed and smiling Ingrams were taken into the house by Marnie. Aubrey followed them and for a few seconds Miranda found herself alone with Roger. Not knowing what to say to him, she turned to follow the others and found him barring her way.

'We'll be talking business for the rest of the afternoon,' he said quietly but firmly. 'May I suggest you stay out here. You can wander in the gardens if you like, do anything you wish. I regret I can't provide you with a companion. Chuck isn't here.'

'Where is he?' she asked innocently. 'And where is his father?'

'Their whereabouts is no concern of yours. Forget them,' he replied brusquely.

'Perhaps Mr Ingram might need me. Sometimes he likes me to take notes of business discussions,' she objected, sensing that he did not wish her to know anything about the particular discussion which was going to take place in the house.

'I know he does,' he said drily. 'He uses you when there's no tape recorder available so that he has evidence to use later. But not this time, Miranda. This time I give the orders and this time there'll be no record of what anyone says. Please make yourself comfortable.'

He turned and went into the cool dim interior of the old house. A little hurt by his coolness, Miranda lingered at the edge of the patio looking down at the small cove at the foot of the cliffs on which the house was built. It was edged by white sand and shaded by long-stemmed palms. On that hot airless day it looked inviting and she longed to go swimming there.

A small wizened dark woman appeared and began to clear away the dishes and the remains of the food. She was helped by a younger woman who smiled at Miranda and

144

introduced herself as Rosie Williams, the sister of Kit. She had once been a nurse in London, she told Miranda, but had returned to Fortuga at Roger's request to be a companion and nurse to Marnie.

For a while they talked about London and then Miranda asked Rosie how she could get down to the cove.

'There's a path twisting down through the shrubbery,' said Rosie. 'But take care if you go swimming and don't go beyond those two rocky points.'

Thanking her, Miranda collected the beach bag which she had brought with her and wandered along the path which led from the patio through the flowering bushes which tumbled down to the shore. Sitting down under one of the palm trees, she removed her skirt and blouse ready to swim or to sunbathe, but before doing either she wanted to read the letter from Aunt Clara again.

Her aunt had obviously been in a very disturbed state of mind when she had written, for she had started the letter abruptly without any greeting.

'Soon after you left Dottie began to behave very strangely, staying out late every night in spite of my objections. Then the Friday of your first week away she didn't come home at all. I was beginning to get worried on Saturday when there was no sign of her, but before I could take any action I received a phone call from her to say she was in Brighton with Joe and that they had been married that morning by special licence.

'I don't know what to say to you, my dear, by way of sympathy. I told Dottie she must explain herself to you face to face when you return. She's not at all repentant and says she's loved Joe for some time and knew that he preferred her to you, although he was reluctant at first to take any step which might hurt you.

'In many ways I'm glad it's her he has married and not you, because I'm convinced you wouldn't have been happy with him.'

Miranda did not read any more and the letter fell from

145

Fancy

her fingers as she stared unseeingly at the bright blue Caribbean Sea twinkling under the afternoon sun.

Joe had married Dottie and not herself, so that when she returned to England he would not be waiting at the airport for her, to greet her with outstretched arms and to say how much he had missed her and to insist that they be married instantly! The rushed romantic wedding had been for her sister, not for her!

Miranda's white teeth punished her soft lower lip as she realised that for almost two years she had been living in a fool's paradise, imagining that Joe was in love with her, hoping that one day he would throw his innate caution to the winds and rush her to the altar. But it had taken a less inhibited person than herself to stampede him into taking any action, and her own sister had been that person.

Oddly enough she had no feeling of pain because Dottie had deceived her. All her criticism was for herself for having imposed upon herself a sort of bondage by imagining that she was in love with Joe and that he was in love with her. Sitting there quietly beside the glittering blue sea, thousands of miles away from home, she could see quite clearly that he had known better than she had that they had not been in love with each other. He had tried to tell her before she had left by saying that her absence would give them both a chance to find out if they were meant for each other.

He had been wise, much wiser than she had been. His hesitancy, his strict routine visits, his brief unrousing kisses had all been signs that he had not loved her. He had never courted her, but she had been too naïve, too wrapped up in romantic daydreams to read the signs correctly.

Now she was free of that self-imposed bondage, free to love where she chose. Free to love Roger if she wished. No, not Roger, because he didn't take love seriously as she did. For him it was a game he played with someone who caught his fancy, an ephemeral relationship which made no demands. There would be danger in loving him.

Miranda sprang to her feet and ran over the soft sand out into the smoothly rolling water. Raising her arms above her head, she dived into a swirling, greenish curving breaker, then surfaced. Ahead of her was another breaker, rolling towards the shore, and she dived into that too.

As usual the water was softly buoyant and caressed her limbs invitingly, tempting her to swim onwards, borne along by the regular rhythm of the waves. At last she turned and floated on her back. She could see the shore, a narrow curve of pale sand backed by the lush green foliage of the cliffside. Above it the sturdy white walls of the old part of the house glinted with yellow light, reflecting the sun.

She knew now why Roger did not want to sell his inheritance. Having seen it and how Marnie had preserved the house and had developed the estate she could understand why he did not want to part with it. Mr Ingram would have no luck today, and that meant the *Sea Quest* would leave Fortuga tomorrow and would carry the Ingrams and herself to another island. It meant saying good-bye to Gallant's Fancy which she had seen for the first time today. It would mean saying good-bye to Roger whom she felt she had known always.

Tears blurred the scene before her. She shook them away, aware suddenly that the water was colder, less buoyant, and that it was pulling her sideways. Looking round, she saw that she had done what Rosie had warned her not to do. She had swum beyond the two points of rock which protected the cove from the open sea. She was caught in a current which was carrying her away down the coast.

Frantically she began to swim back towards the cove, using an overarm crawl stroke, but after about ten minutes she had to stop and tread water because she felt tired. She had made no progress against the current at all. A wave came up and slapped her in the face. She gulped and sank immediately, came up spluttering and started to swim again desperately, feeling the current pulling at her limbs, making them useless, and knowing deep in her heart that she hadn't a chance of survival because she wasn't strong enough.

Wearily she turned on her back and floated. It was difficult and she went under twice, conscious of a leaden dullness in her legs as if their muscles had cramped. She tried to move them and sank again.

As she fought her way to the surface, her heart and lungs ready to burst, she saw something which looked like dark red seaweed streaming in the water above her. She surfaced and felt hands seize her and an arm like an iron band went round her. A voice said,

'I'm not going to let you drown, not now that you've come to Gallant's Fancy, Miranda, Gallant's Fancy, Miranda...'

She was having that crazy dream again. The only way to get rid of it was to turn over and go to sleep. That was what she needed, sleep. If only she could get rid of the iron band holding her. She struggled, turned over, closed her eyes and all went dark.

She knew nothing more until nausea heaved in her stomach. Someone pulled her to an upright position and she retched painfully. Vaguely she realised she was on the beach. She could hear voices, then someone wrapped her in a blanket and she was lifted up. She looked up and saw, rather hazily, a dark face above hers and a pair of light eyes glinting down at her. *The devil and not the deep blue sea had won after all*, she thought wildly. The dark face smiled and came into proper focus and she recognised who was carrying her. Aubrey Vincent.

'What happened?' a thin weary voice asked.

'You swam too far and were caught by the current which sweeps along this coast of the island. Don't talk. You're very tired. You'll soon be in the house and in bed.'

'Oh, but I must go to the yacht.' That silly reedy voice she could hear must be hers!

'Not now,' he replied. 'Don't worry, little one. You'll be

148

taken care of by Marnie. She loves to have a chick to fuss over.'

He carried her all the way up the twisting path, through the house and up the stairs, and Miranda marvelled at his strength. She could hear Marnie speaking behind her and then in front of her. She was taken into a big room with a high decorated ceiling and placed carefully on an enormous bed. A door closed and two people appeared beside the bed: Marnie, her face drawn into anxious lines and her blind, scarred sea-blue eyes uncovered, blank and staring, and Rosie Williams, tall and competent-looking, her brown face composed and serious.

Rosie rolled her big brown eyes and clicked her tongue. 'My, that was a near thing! You didn't pay attention to what I said, missy, and you almost drowned,' she said. 'I'm going to undress you now and wash you and put you into one of Miss Gallant's nighties until your own things are brought from the yacht. Then you're going to have a nice long sleep.'

Miranda heard that funny thin voice apologising for being a nuisance and causing trouble.

'It's no trouble, honey,' soothed Marnie, her hand going out unerringly to smooth back Miranda's wet tangled hair. 'Relax now and let Rosie do everything for you. She's the best nurse in the Caribbean.'

Rosie was gentle yet firm and Miranda was too tired to object any more. Almost before Rosie had finished arranging the bedclothes about her after washing and changing her, she fell asleep, having decided that the picture on the ceiling of the room was of Cupid, the God of Love.

CHAPTER SIX

REDDISH-BROWN seaweed floated before her and she watched it, fascinated by its undulating movements. It changed subtly, growing finer in texture. It was hair, chestnut in colour. It parted and a face appeared, sculptured in bronze. The eyes were closed and it reminded her of a death mask. *Roger.* The name screamed through her mind. Miranda turned her head, opened her eyes and saw Marnie sitting in a chair beside the bed, placidly moving her hands over a book of Braille which was open on her knee.

Her heart still pounding after the nightmare, Miranda let her gaze drift round the room, then up to the ceiling. The sight of Cupid shooting an arrow at her calmed her. He was a chubby, softly rounded Cupid and had several half-dressed nymphs in attendance. Amazed that anyone should have wanted such a painting on the ceiling of their bedroom, she glanced towards the window. It was open, but screened to prevent flying insects from invading the room. Through it she could see the hot blue of the sky and could hear very faintly the soft hiss of waves falling upon sand. Then came another sound, much closer, in the house, the clear notes of a piano being played.

She glanced at the woman sitting beside the bed. The straight sun-tanned features were calm, the mouth faintly smiling, the eyes blank and unfocussed.

'Marnie,' she said, and was relieved to hear that her voice was normal again.

Marnie's hands stopped moving. She closed the book and laid it aside on a small occasional table which had a mother-of-pearl top and delicately curved legs. The sight of it caused Miranda to look more closely at the other furniture in the room. It was all made like that, the chairs having oval backs and tapestry seats, their wooden legs and frames

150

picked out in gold-leaf paint.

'Ah, so you're awake at last, honey, and feeling hungry, I'm sure,' said Marnie cheerfully. 'You've slept ever since Rosie and I left you. There's nothing like sleep to restore you after a catastrophe. It heals the nerves, as I should know.'

'Did you sleep a long time after the accident which damaged your eyes?' asked Miranda tentatively.

'For a very long time. In fact it was several days before I realised fully that I couldn't see.'

'How did it happen?'

'It's rather a complicated story,' sighed Marnie, 'and not one I'm fond of telling, because it makes me appear rather silly and naïve. Once I was a student of chemistry—I even managed to get a degree in the science at Cambridge. When I returned to live here I had my own laboratory in the house. One day someone I had annoyed very much picked up a phial of sulphuric acid and threw it at me.'

Miranda gasped, shocked that anyone could behave in such a violent manner, then recalled Dawn throwing the remains of her drink at Roger. It seemed that the Gallants had a knack of rousing others to act violently.

'How awful!' she remarked.

'Yes, it was awful and extremely painful, but you see she was a simple soul and didn't know the phial's contents were dangerous, and she was very, very angry with me. When I had time to think about it afterwards I realised she had every right to be.'

'Why? What had you done to her?' asked Miranda, still finding it difficult to believe that anyone as kindly and as good-humoured as Marnie seemed to be could irritate anyone, and then reminding herself that she had seen Chuck once almost hit Roger.

Marnie sighed again, placed one hand over the other on her lap and leaned back in her chair.

'This is the part which goes against me,' she said. 'Ten years ago I was very naïve, disgustingly innocent about a lot of things and terribly moral and upright. I was a self-righteous prig who had no hesitation in telling others when I thought they were doing wrong.'

'Who did you think was doing something wrong?'

'A woman called Josephine. My cousin Thomas had picked her up on one of his jaunts to Martinique. His wife, Rita, had left him, taking the children with her, and he decided he needed a housekeeper. He thought Josephine would do very well. She was tall and beautiful, and I need hardly tell you she was more to Thomas than his house-keeper.'

Marnie paused and frowned. Miranda waited. At last she was going to solve the mystery of Josephine.

'I'm telling you this, Miranda, because I have the impression that, like I was ten years ago, you are also rather naïve and innocent and that possibly you hold some puritan views,' continued Marnie. 'I learned my code of morals at the knee of my grandmother, my father's mother, who had been the daughter of the manse in a Scottish town. She came out to the Caribbean to teach music and married a roistering Gallant for her pains. She was strong, self-reliant and deeply religious.'

'Like my Aunt Clara,' murmured Miranda, and Marnie smiled.

'So you have your mentor too,' she commented. 'Then you might find a lesson to be learned in my story. It will give you an insight into behaviour. Never assume that everyone thinks as you do or as your Aunt Clara does. I used to believe that a man didn't kiss a woman until he wanted to show her that he loved her and wanted to marry her—a romantic outlook, and one which I had no desire to change. It was summer time and Roger was home for a vacation from the university where he was studying musical composition. He was twenty-one, a grown man, but for me he was still the young brother I had played with, clever, determined, dedicated to his music but with a strange propensity for mischief.'

152

Marnie closed her eyes as if by doing so she could see into the past, and Miranda shifted her position, sitting up in bed and curling her legs under her.

'He spent his holiday in the usual way, swimming, diving, water-skiing, sailing, or just loafing around with old friends. Then I noticed he often went to Gallant's Folly. I was bothered, because he and Thomas had never been good friends, and I began to wonder what mischief he was up to. I heard quite by accident that he was often with Josephine and that they went swimming and sunbathing together. One day I came across them. They were in each other's arms, kissing.'

Miranda had a vivid mental picture of Roger and Dawn kissing on the beach, remembered the shock which had quivered through her body and relived the moment.

'I was shocked,' said Marnie. 'I shouldn't have been, but I was. Then I was afraid of what Thomas might do if he found out. I was also afraid of what Josephine might do to my brother, who was younger than she was and who was, so I believed, as innocent as I was. It was then that I made my big mistake. Instead of talking to Roger about it I asked Josephine to come and see me. She came, flaunting her amazing beauty in the laboratory.'

'What did you say to her?'

'Oh, I was very much the plantation owner's daughter telling a servant to keep her place,' said Marnie, self-disparagingly. 'I told her to leave my brother alone, and she laughed at me in amazement. Strangely disturbed by her laughter, I warned her that I would tell Thomas what she was doing when his back was turned and that I would have her turned off the island. She lost her temper, because she was frightened, and picked up the nearest thing to hurl at me. While I was fighting with the pain she ran from the room. She was never seen here again.'

'And were you right about her?'

'No, not really,' Marnie's voice was very dry. 'I learned too late that my young brother was quite capable of looking after himself. Far from being led astray by a practised coquette he had merely been indulging in one of his favourite pastimes, tormenting Thomas.'

'Playing pirates?'

'In a way, yes. He told me that he had found Josephine attractive and different, and he had kissed her to find out what she was like. There was nothing in that one kiss, but I had to see them. I understand now, but when he told me I was too ill and frightened by what had happened to me and it was a long time before I could forgive him. He was very patient with me and stayed here until I was well enough to travel to consult specialists in the States and in Britain to find out if anything could be done to restore my sight. He refused to go back to his university. We travelled for about three years, during which time I had two operations with only partial success. After the last one I decided I was wasting my time and Roger's. I came back here determined to work to develop Fortuga. But Roger wouldn't stay here. He went off on his own. Then he wrote that song and his success as a composer of light music was assured.'

'He's always felt responsible for what happened to you,' said Miranda.

'Did he tell you that?' Marnie sounded surprised.

'Not directly, but I heard him tell Juanita and Chuck that he couldn't sell Gallant's Fancy because it was your home and that if you went to live anywhere else you would wither and die, and then he would have that on his conscience as well as your blindness.'

'It's quite true. I don't think I could live anywhere else because I've put so much of myself into the place,' said Marnie, but she looked very distressed. 'It's become so important to me that I'm in danger of forgetting that it's his home too and belongs to him by right of inheritance. I'd no idea he felt like that. He hasn't been here much during the past few years and I've heard gossip about him which I haven't liked. When he has come to see me he's seemed the same, not quite so lively perhaps, but lovable, often vague

154

and absent-minded when working on his music. He's composing now. Can you hear the piano?'

'Yes.' Miranda had wondered why one phrase was being played over and over again with slight variations.

Marnie stood up.

'That's enough of my problems for today,' she said with her warm smile. 'Now I'm going to ask Rosie to prepare a meal for you and tell Roger you're awake. He would like to come and see you. He'd walk in on you without so much as a knock on the door, but I told him you would have to be asked first. Can he come and see you?'

Miranda smiled a little, thinking that Marnie was much more old-fashioned than herself. Then she remembered dark red hair floating in the water above her, an arm around her like an iron band, a voice saying that she mustn't drown. She had to see Roger to thank him for rescuing her.

'I would like to see him, please. I have to thank him,' she said simply, and Marnie smiled and nodded before leaving the room.

When the door had closed Miranda lay back on the pillows and gazed at the fat pink Cupid and his bevy of nymphs. She thought about Roger who played at love and who had to kiss a woman to find out what she was like. He had kissed her and had found out that she was naïve and innocent and had lost interest in her, just as Dawn had said.

She sighed. She understood only too well why Marnie had told her the story of Josephine. It was to be regarded as a warning not to take Roger seriously.

Lost in thought, she lay there, her hair spread out on the white pillow in a profusion of dark shining silk. Feeling the warmth of the day, she had pushed aside the light covers. So deep in thought was she, still staring at the ceiling, that she did not hear the door open quietly and she jumped when a voice spoke, lazily mockingly.

' ' "A sweet disorder in the dress

155

Kindles in clothes a wantonness," ' said Roger.

'Oh!' Miranda's gasp was expressive and she sat up suddenly, pulling the sheet up to her chin and making him laugh. He was standing at the foot of the bed, his hair glowing like a dark flame in that room of pastel shades, his eyes shimmering with green light.

'For a churchman Robert Herrick had an unerring eye for all that's attractive in a woman and had a marvellous ability for expressing it without offending,' he said.

'I didn't hear you come in,' she stammered, her cheeks rosy at the thought of him standing there surveying her without her knowing, as she had lain half in and half out of the voluminous nightdress which belonged to Marnie.

'I know you didn't. You were too busy admiring Cupid. You must know every fold and curve of his body by now,' he teased.

'Who had him painted?' she asked.

'The wife of the Roger Gallant who built the front part of the house when part of the old Spanish house was burned down. She was from Martinique, a member of one of the old French plantation families. She had visited Versailles. When she came here as Roger's bride she had this room decorated and furnished as the bridal suite in the style which she most admired. The furniture in here is all genuine French stuff. It's survived the ravages of time and climate, to say nothing of the antics of the lively Gallant children who were born and nursed in this room, remarkably well, don't you think?'

'It's a lovely room,' she replied shyly.

He had come to the side of the bed and she saw he was carrying her beach bag. Immediately Miranda thought of the letter she had been reading on the beach before she had gone swimming and wondered if it had blown away.

'I've brought this,' he murmured, placing it on the bed. 'It was on the beach.'

To her surprise he sat on the side of the enormous four-poster bed, quite close to her, and his narrowed gaze flicked over her face and hair assessingly. She wished suddenly that she had not agreed to see him. Dressed as she was in the large nightgown which would keep slipping off her shoulders, she could not let go of the sheet and had to sit up with it clutched around her.

'If you lie back against your pillows you'll be much more comfortable, Miranda,' he suggested gently, showing he was aware of her predicament.

She leaned back gingerly, still clutching the sheet. Then finding he was right she relaxed her hold on it because it stayed in place once she was lying down.

'That's better,' he observed. 'How are you feeling?'

'A little light-headed,' she squeaked.

It was the truth, but she wasn't sure whether the strange whirling feeling she was experiencing was due to lack of food, to the results of almost drowning or to his nearness. No man had the right to be as attractive as he was, she thought indignantly, very much aware of the clean taut line of his jaw, of the smooth golden-brown of throat and chest contrasted against the faded blue cotton shirt which he was wearing and which was open to the waist as if he'd thrown it on hurriedly before coming up to see her. Surely the poem he had quoted applied just as much to him as it had to her. The disorder in his clothing drew attention to his physical attraction, and she had a longing to slip a hand inside his shirt to feel the beat of his heart.

The longing alarmed her, making her even more shy of him, although she appeared outwardly cool and composed.

'Thank you from rescuing me,' she said.

'What makes you think I did?' he replied coolly, throwing her into confusion. She had no way of telling from the expression on his face whether he had rescued her or not. She had only the memory of hair floating like reddish-brown seaweed in the greenish water and of a voice urging her not to drown. But that could have been a dream.

'I thought I heard you talking to me. You said . . .'

'You have a powerful imagination, Miranda,' he interrupted her drily. 'I said nothing. I was too busy trying to keep you afloat until Aubrey was able to help me heave you into the speedboat. You were determined to lie face downwards and drown. Why did you want to drown?'

The curt question startled her. He was looking at her with a grim, cold expression in his eyes, almost as if he didn't approve of her.

'I didn't want to drown. I swam too far, that's all.'

'Even after being warned by Rosie?' He sounded sceptical, and she was indignant.

'I didn't realise how far I'd swum until I felt the current pulling at me. I tried to swim back, but I was too tired. Honestly, Roger, I had no reason for wanting to drown—and anyway, I would never do such a thing. It would be wrong,' she stated vehemently.

'I see,' he murmured, and his eyelashes veiled his eyes.

'I'm sorry to have caused so much trouble,' she offered humbly, 'and I'm truly grateful you and Aubrey rescued me. As soon as I can get up I'll go back to *Sea Quest*.'

Roger looked up. His eyes were quite cold.

'You can't. *Sea Quest* left early this morning.'

'Oh! What shall I do? When will the Ingrams come back? What happened? Why did they leave without me?' she asked, her voice rising almost hysterically. She felt deserted, completely alone, at the mercy of this man whose nearness affected her senses so strangely.

'Having failed to buy the Gallant estate Ingram was in a hurry to get to Cane Island to clinch a deal there,' said Roger. 'He has to do something to justify the expense of the cruise he's just taken through the islands. One can hardly blame him. A man who's as accustomed to success as he is doesn't take kindly to defeat.'

'How did you defeat him?' Miranda asked tremulously.

'He capitulated when I told him that Gallant's Folly had been bought by another syndicate.'

It was strange how that downward curve to one corner of his mouth made it more attractive. She wanted to trace the

158

curve with her finger and then to kiss the corner gently until he turned and plundered her mouth with his kisses.

Miranda swallowed hard. What was the matter with her? Why was she having such crazy, abandoned thoughts?

'Which syndicate?' she asked shakily, trying to keep her mind on the course of the conversation.

'Marnie and Aubrey. They're partners in a new enterprise to develop Fortuga as a tourist resort.'

'But how did you persuade Thomas to sell his half to them?'

'I kidnapped Dawn and held her to ransom,' he replied, quite seriously, but this time the corner of his mouth didn't curve downwards. Instead it twitched with amusement.

'How?'

'I gave her the fare to New York and the name of an agent there who would give her a start in a new career as a singer. She needed no second urging. She left as soon as she could get a plane from Grenada to San Juan. I wouldn't tell Thomas where she'd gone until he agreed to sell Gallant's Fancy to Marnie and Aubrey. When he learned how much they were prepared to give him for the place he gave in at once. An agreement was signed here the night before last and he and Chuck left early the next morning bound for New York.'

'Pirate!' she accused, and he raised his eyebrows in surprise.

'I suppose so,' he conceded. 'Desperate situations often call for desperate measures. I didn't have enough money to buy Thomas off myself. All I could do was stall until we reached Fortuga.'

'Why did you have to do that?'

'I knew what Marnie and Aubrey had in mind for the Folly, but I wasn't sure whether they had been able to raise the money, so I couldn't say anything to Thomas. Fortunately he'd spun that tale about the old entail to Ingram. He'd said that he would have to raise his price in order to pay for the breaking of the entail. Ingram wouldn't agree unless he could have Gallant's Fancy as well, when he heard from me that it was a much better site than the Folly. I knew that the entail was worth nothing and wouldn't stand up in a court of law. It was only a gentleman's agreement made over two centuries ago. It was a case of playing Thomas and Ingram off against one another until I'd been able to establish some means of bargaining with Thomas.'

'But why did you decide to use Dawn?'

'It wasn't until I learned from you why Ingram had set her on to me that it occurred to me that I could take a leaf out of his book of rules and use it with effect. I knew that Thomas had made her promise to give up singing when he married her. He's very possessive and he didn't like the idea of sharing her with an audience. All I had to do was give her an opportunity to sing, which I did in Antigua. Then there was no holding her back. Once I'd persuaded her to go to New York without telling Thomas, I had the means of bargaining with him. Are you sorry Ingram and Transmarine lost?'

'Not really. I can see why you want to keep Gallant's Fancy and I understand much better now why you think Fortuga should be developed by the people who live here. Marnie has done wonders,' said Miranda.

There was a little silence. His explaining done, Roger didn't seem to have anything more to say to her. He put a hand in his pocket and pulled out an envelope and handed it to her.

'Ingram left this for you,' he said curtly.

'Thank you.' She slit the envelope open and a cheque fell out. There was no explanatory note with it.

'I expect they'll come back this way to collect me. They can't go back to San Juan without me,' she said with more confidence than she was feeling, hoping he would reassure her.

'I expect so,' he said vaguely, and she had the impression that his mind had wandered off along paths which she could not follow. 'Meanwhile,' he added, 'you are welcome to stay here, to recover from an unpleasant experience and have a short holiday. What will happen when you return to London?'

He was being polite, showing an interest in her future she was sure he didn't feel.

'I expect I'll go into the typing pool again. I don't seem to be cut out to be a high-powered private secretary. I become too involved with people and take sides,' she confessed.

He slanted her a quizzical sidelong glance and she blushed.

'I'm glad you were on my side,' he murmured, and rose to his feet. 'I'd better leave you now or Marnie will be complaining that it isn't seemly for me to be here alone with you in this room of all rooms, especially since you're wearing a nightdress. She's conveniently forgotten that I've seen you many times with far less clothing on when you've been swimming. She's a born Victorian and has a pretty severe code of morals.'

'Which you don't share?' dared Miranda. Although he had spoken lightly there was an undercurrent of sarcasm in his voice and she guessed that he and Marnie had had a disagreement that morning about whether he should come to the bedroom.

He raised a haughty eyebrow at her.

'I have a code of morals, but it belongs to this century and not to the last, and I hope it's more realistic. By sticking to her own outdated code Marnie is hurting not only other people but herself as well. Take this thing between her and Aubrey. They should be living together. They should be more than business partners, they should be marriage partners. But she has some lofty idealistic notion that he shouldn't be saddled with a blind wife. He has some chivalrous idea that he isn't good enough to be her husband. Both of them are so full of consideration for the other that they're likely to spend the rest of their lives living apart, pining with unrequited love. Hypocrites, both of them, to

161

my way of thinking. They make me tired.'

His voice thickened with disgust and he turned away to walk over to the window to look out. Amazed at his sudden outburst, Miranda lay blinking at his back.

'Why does Aubrey think he isn't good enough for her?' she asked.

He swung round to look at her across the room.

'Because his father was a sailor on a Dutch freighter and his mother was probably descended from slaves. He seems to think that because she's a Gallant of Fortuga and has a family tree and lives in a beautiful house, she's above him, which is a lot of nonsense! The Gallants are no better than anyone else, as you've seen for yourself,' he replied, still disgusted. 'Love such as theirs should be consummated, not wasted, and they needn't be afraid of prejudice because they don't have to live anywhere else but Fortuga, where prejudice is non-existent. Thanks to me, Marnie can't live anywhere else.'

Bitterness edged his voice and drove lines down his lean cheeks, making him look older.

'She told me about Josephine,' said Miranda, wanting to ease the pain she knew he felt because he held himself responsible for Marnie's blindness. 'She doesn't blame you any more. She can see it was her own fault for being too self-righteous and for interfering.'

'It was that antiquated moral code of hers,' he muttered, giving her an underbrowed wary glance. 'And I dare say she told you the story in order to point a moral to you.'

Irritation flitted across his sun-tanned face and he strode across to the door.

'I've no more time for gossiping,' he said curtly. 'I have work to do.'

'I heard you playing the piano.'

'I was trying out a melody for the ballet. My melody for Miranda.' The glance he gave her now was neither wary nor irritated, but mocked her gently.

'For Shakespeare's Miranda?' she queried, her breath

162

catching in her throat.

'For who else?' he countered tauntingly. 'Please feel at home here for a while and don't be in too much of a hurry to go swimming. Tell me when you're ready to brave the ocean again and I'll go with you.'

The lilting melody, with its subtle Spanish-American beat overlaid by a sound which owed its origins to English folk music, haunted the house for the next few days. They were days of sunshine and somnolence for Miranda as she recovered from almost drowning and wandered around learning the secrets of the house called Gallant's Fancy.

It was, she discovered, a house with a split personality, like the music which Roger had composed for Shakespeare's Miranda. The front of it, built by the Gallant who had been a successful plantation owner and distiller of rum, a trader who had owned his own fleet of schooners at the beginning of the nineteenth century, was full of light. Its rooms were lofty and airy. They had a faded elegance into which the mixture of French and English eighteenth-century furniture and Victorian bric-à-brac fitted comfortably. It was easy to imagine the social gatherings which had taken place there and the tall graceful Roger Gallant of the time moving amongst his guests. Miranda's favourite room in that part of the house was her bedroom, the bridal suite of the beautiful French woman from Martinique who had been, according to the family tree Miranda had discovered in the library, the great-great-great-grandmother of Marnie and Roger.

The library or music room, as it was now called, was Miranda's other favourite room, and it was in the other part of the house, the Spanish part, which was dim and cool with rounded arches in thick stone walls, low ceilings and dark beams, wrought iron gateways and screens, tasselled velvet curtains and long low sofas. There, where amber lights kept the shadows at bay during the long warm evenings, she found it easy to imagine the bearded Castilian hidalgo who had first settled on the island and whose daughter had been forced to marry the piratical Englishman who had taken a fancy not only to Fortuga but also to her.

It was in that room amongst the leather-bound volumes which filled the shelves, the old parchment charts of the Caribbean islands, the numerous family portraits and photographs which decorated the white walls, that Roger spent nearly all his time composing the music for a new ballet, occasionally trying out a phrase or a variation on the shining rosewood piano which had been given to him by his grandmother Fiona MacGregor, whose fine Scottish face smiled down benignly on him from her portrait on the wall above the instrument.

Miranda expected the Ingrams to return for her in about ten days, so she settled down intending to make the most of her brief stay. She wrote to Aunt Clara explaining what had happened and enclosed a letter to Dottie and Joe wishing them every happiness. Then she turned her attention to Marnie and Aubrey, spending as much time in the mornings as she could with one or the other. The afternoons belonged to Roger.

True to his promise he went swimming with her, and the swimming sessions were both a delight and a torment to her. Sometimes he was in a mischievous playful mood and would splash her unmercifully or would arrive unseen by her, swim after her under water and surprise her by surfacing suddenly beside her. Other times he was so vague and withdrawn that he might as well not have been there. After swimming they would usually lie side by side on the sand to sunbathe and perhaps, if Roger was in the mood, to talk.

Therein lay the torment. To be so close to him, to know he had only to reach out a hand and touch her, made the afternoons dangerously exciting. But he never did touch her, and soon Miranda forgot the danger and allowed herself to enjoy his company believing that all too soon she would have to say good-bye to him.

Once Aubrey took her to see all that was left of Gallant's

Folly, the house which Thomas had deserted almost ten years ago. It was a poor copy of the other and was built in a bad situation. By now Miranda knew from her study of the family tree that the younger branch of the original Gallant family had died out. There had been other younger sons who had taken over the Folly, but they had either died or given up the place and gone off to live somewhere else. As a result of Thomas's neglect, the groves of coconut and banana palms had grown wild and their fruit lay rotting on the ground and the acreage which had been used for sugarcane was abandoned and scorched by the hot sun.

Marnie and Aubrey planned to knock down the old house and build holiday cottages and restore the land to productivity. The cottages would be for people who wished to have a holiday 'away from it all' and who did not like the organised routines and laid-on entertainment of the big hotels which they could get anywhere.

'It's important to preserve the desert island paradise idea for them while providing adequate shelter and modern amenities,' explained Aubrey as they walked back together through a grove of fruit trees which were Marnie's pride and joy.

'I understand,' said Miranda, 'and it really is a paradise. It's a pity Marnie can't see the results of her farming and landscaping.'

'She can smell and feel,' he replied in his placid way.

Miranda glanced at his dark handsome face and wondered whether Marnie had ever touched it, feeling it with her sensitive fingers in order to 'read' it.

'Even so, her blindness could stand in her way and prevent her from attaining true happiness,' she observed.

'I don't understand, little one. What is true happiness, and why shouldn't Marnie have it? What more could she want from life than to live on Fortuga in a place she loves, doing something she's good at and enjoys?'

'She might like to have a companion, someone she could hold hands with to comfort her in the long lonely nights.'

'Hey, now, wait a minute!' he said in his slow deep voice, stopping in his tracks. Miranda stopped too and turned to face him. The sun shining through the foliage of the trees dappled them with yellow light and birds squawked noisily in the bush. 'Are you trying to tell me that Marnie would like to be loved and that because she's blind that isn't possible?

'Yes. You see, she thinks it wrong to saddle the man she loves with a blind wife, and as she's a very strong-minded and proud woman he'll have to be a very persistent and loving man to make her change her mind.'

'You're sure that's how she's thinking?'

'Quite sure. Roger told me.'

'And he should know, because he has his own share of Gallant stubbornness and pride,' Aubrey murmured musingly. Suddenly he let out a full-throated bellow of laughter. 'A very persistent and loving man,' he repeated after he had stopped laughing. 'That's me, honey-child. I'm the most persistent and the lovingest man on Fortuga. You'll see if I'm not.'

They went on to the house, the small dark-haired English girl and the tall dark man, and their approach was watched with some interest by Roger who happened to be looking out of a window. That evening he invited Aubrey to stay for dinner, and instead of refusing the big man accepted the invitation. After the meal was over they all sat on the patio. Eventually Roger slipped away and soon the piano could be heard, but for once he was playing properly, a nostalgic nocturne by Chopin.

Taking her cue from Roger, Miranda also moved away from the patio, leaving Marnie and Aubrey alone. She walked in the gardens as far as possible from the house and away from the sound of the romantic music which aroused strange yearnings within her.

Next day Marnie was unusually irritable, and after lunch Miranda, feeling sorry for the blind woman, stayed to sit

166

with her in the shade instead of going for her swim with Roger.

'Aubrey is very strong,' she mused. 'I'm still amazed at the way he was able to carry me all the way up the slope from the beach and to the bedroom without stopping once. He's handsome too.'

Marnie's head turned in her direction, but she said nothing.

'His eyes are grey, crystal clear, but perhaps they look that way because his skin is dark,' continued Miranda.

Still Marnie said nothing, but her hands, which were resting on the arms of her chair, tightened.

'He's rather a sensitive person for one so big and strong and his sensitivity could get in the way of him attaining true happiness,' continued Miranda.

'What do you mean by true happiness? What is that?' Marnie's voice was sharp.

'Living with the person you love for the rest of your life,' replied Miranda serenely. 'Sharing everything with her.'

'And why can't Aubrey do that?'

'Because he believes he isn't good enough for the woman he loves.'

'Any woman should be proud to be loved by a man like Aubrey,' asserted Marnie. 'How foolish of him! Wait until this evening. I'll tell him a thing or two!'

Marnie didn't wait for Roger to ask Aubrey to dinner that night. She invited him herself, and neither Roger nor Miranda bothered to go and sit out on the patio after the meal was over, but left the shadowy fragrant place to the other two.

In the days that followed it was obvious that the relationship between the two business partners had entered a new phase. They tended to linger longer in each other's company and found ways of being alone together. Whether Roger noticed any difference Miranda could not be sure, and she was unable to ask him because, to her secret disappointment, he had stopped swimming with her and took his daily dip in the ocean later in the afternoon, just before dinner.

He was, she supposed, too absorbed in his music. She hadn't realised that composing could be such hard concentrated work, and she said so one afternoon when she returned from the sea, having swum alone.

'You're seeing something rarely seen by any of us,' said Marnie drily. 'Roger at work. I know he has to finish the ballet before a certain date. Also he's determined that the music shall be a success. It's been good having him here even if he has been working all the time. I have you to thank for him being here at all.'

'Me?' Miranda was astounded, surprised that Roger's presence in his own home had anything to do with her.

'Yes. He told me he wouldn't have gone on the cruise after learning why Ingram had invited him, but he heard from Juanita that if he left you might lose your job for inadvertently telling him of Ingram's intentions. I'm glad he stayed on the yacht and came here, otherwise Thomas might have tricked us as he did once before. I hope you're enjoying your stay here.'

'I couldn't do otherwise,' said Miranda sincerely. 'It's such a beautiful place, and you've been very kind to me. The Ingrams should be returning soon to pick me up. It's exactly two weeks since they left.'

'But, honey, they aren't coming back for you.'

'Not coming back? They must. How am I to get to San Juan to catch the plane to London?' Miranda felt panic rising within her. Surely Marnie was wrong and had misunderstood the arrangements?

'Didn't Mr Ingram leave you a note explaining?' asked Marnie. She was looking very bewildered.

'No. There was only a cheque in the envelope, rather more than I'd expected for the month.'

Suspicion was forming at the back of her mind. It grew quickly, mushrooming like a cloud of dust stirred up by a violent explosion.

'Who told you that the Ingrams aren't coming back?' she asked.

'Roger. After he and Aubrey had brought you ashore he told the Ingrams you weren't fit to sail with them that day. Apparently Mr Ingram was very irritable and said he couldn't wait for you to recover. He wrote out that cheque and we assumed that he included a note explaining to you why he'd left and giving you instructions. He told Roger that you were to return to London on your own and that he had no further use for your services.'

'Oh!' Miranda was on her feet. 'He didn't tell me. He tricked me!' she exclaimed, but she didn't specify whom she meant by 'he'.

'Do you think so?' asked Marnie in a puzzled way. 'It seems straightforward to me. I've loved having you to stay here. It's been good for me to have someone young and fresh from the outside world to keep me company, to be my eyes and tell me the size and colour of the fruit, the colour of Aubrey's eyes.' Her voice shook a little. 'Please don't think you have to leave because the Ingrams aren't coming back for you. You can stay here, for ever if you like. I would like that.'

'I must go. I must go home!' cried Miranda, afraid of the love which she could feel reaching out to her, binding her.

She ran indoors and went up to her room. There, under the pink, blue and gold ceiling, she paced back and forth, caught in a storm of anger which the knowlege of Roger's trickery had roused. She hadn't felt like that since he'd kissed her on the beach in the Virgin Islands. Then she had fought with him. She wanted to fight him now, to shout at him, to inflict some wound, yet she knew that to do so would only make him laugh because he dearly loved a fight.

From the music room the clear notes of the melody which formed the basis of the music for Miranda, came quite clearly as she paused outside the double doors and braced herself to enter. It was almost dinner time and she had changed into the long blue skirt and sheer frilly blouse which she had worn that first night in San Juan.

Taking a deep breath to try and cool the fiery feeling which was raging inside her, she opened one of the doors quietly, stepped into the room and closed the door behind her. Apart from the single lamp on the table where Roger was sitting the room was dark. In the shadowy recesses the gilt lettering on old books glinted, the golden velvety sheen of the sofa gleamed seductively and the grand piano shimmered with deep rose-coloured light.

Roger must have been swimming after all, quite recently, for his hair was damp, sleeked back behind his ears as he bent over some sheets of music manuscript. As was his habit when working in the heat of the day he was clad only in white cotton pants, belted low on his hips, and the bare sun-beaten skin of his back and shoulders gleamed in the amber light as he picked up a sparkling cut-glass tumbler from the table and sipped the iced rum and water which it contained.

'Roger,' she said, trying not to be diverted by the ripple of muscles beneath smooth bronzed skin, pleased because her voice sounded cool and composed. 'Why did you tell me that the Ingrams would be returning to Fortuga to collect me?'

He placed the glass down on the desk and half-turned to glance at her.

'As far as I can remember I didn't,' he replied calmly.

In the light from the lamp his eyes sparkled with icy brilliance as they flicked over the dark blue skirt, white ruffled blouse, peach-bloomed cheeks and dark hair of the young woman who was standing by the piano. Outwardly she seemed calm, but his sharp glance noticed that her eyes had darkened almost to purple and that her slight breasts rose and fell rapidly, causing the frills which edged the deep V-neckline of her blouse to flutter slightly.

'You asked me if they were coming back and I didn't answer your question,' he said quietly. 'Later you assumed they were coming back and seemed quite happy in your assumption, so I left it at that.'

He shrugged his shoulders as if the workings of her mind were beyond his comprehension and turned back to the table to pick up his pen.

'But you knew they weren't coming back and you didn't tell me. You tricked me into staying here,' she accused angrily, the smouldering fire within her stirred into a leaping flame by his indifferent attitude.

He laid down his pen again and stood up to lean against the table so that he could face her.

'All right, I tricked you into staying here,' he conceded blandly. 'Are you sorry you stayed? Haven't you liked being here?'

'You know I've liked being here. But that isn't the point. I would never have imposed upon yours and Marnie's hospitality for such a long time if I'd known the Ingrams wouldn't be returning.'

'If imposing upon our hospitality is all that's worrying you, forget it. Hospitality is something which the people of this island pride themselves on. You've been very welcome, Miranda,' he returned smoothly.

He was evading the issue, keeping his temper and offering pleasant placating words in return for her accusation.

'Why didn't you tell me?' she insisted.

Again he lifted his shoulders in a shrug as if tired of the argument.

'I intended to do so,' he admitted, 'but you were weak after almost drowning and the message which Ingram left with me to pass on to you wasn't very kind.'

'What did he say?' she demanded.

'Do you really want to know?' he parried.

'Of course I do,' she replied. 'You had no right to withhold it from me in the first place.'

'Very well, then I shall tell you,' he said, and his voice was several degrees colder. 'He said that you'd been remarkably useless during the cruise and quite incapable of

171

carrying out the duties he had set you to do.'

'Oh! That was unjust of him. I did all his letters and took notes!' exclaimed Miranda, her eyes sparkling with anger.

'I rather think it wasn't those duties to which he was referring,' said Roger with a wry twist to his mouth. 'Have you forgotten that he asked you to try and influence me and at the same time keep Chuck from getting too impatient? You failed to do either, in his eyes, so he told me. Oh, he was in a bad mood and had to find a scapegoat for his failure. He chose you, and when I suggested that you should stay here and rest until you'd recovered from almost drowning he was extremely unpleasant and made some nasty remarks about your association with me which I prefer not to repeat to you. Then he handed me that cheque for you. It was in lieu of notice. He sacked you there and then. You no longer work for Transmarine, Miranda.'

She stared at him in consternation, unable to say anything, wondering what Aunt Clara would say when she learned that her most diligent niece had been sacked for failing to do her duties and, what was more, sacked without reference and without a good name.

'I found it impossible to pass on such a callous message to you when I knew you'd already received one bad blow that day,' said Roger more gently.

Miranda groped in her memory. What blow had she received that day when she had nearly drowned? Of course, she had received Aunt Clara's letter with its news about Dottie and Joe.

'How do you know I had?' she demanded, feeling anger rising again.

'I found Aunt Clara's letter,' he replied, and she thought she saw pity soften the usual hard brilliance of his eyes.

'And you read it,' she accused.

'And I read it,' he agreed.

Not only had he tricked her into staying in his home for two weeks, but he had known she had been sacked and,

172

worst of all, he had also known of her humiliation at the hands of her sister and Joe. He had known too much and he had said nothing. Anger was whipped into a blaze which made her reckless of what she said to him.

'Oh, is there nothing you won't stoop to? Are you so unprincipled that you'll even read a person's private letters?' she stormed.

A faint frown darkened his face momentarily, an indication that he might possibly become annoyed if she continued to throw accusations at him.

'It was blowing about the beach. I read it thinking it might give me some indication why you had decided to swim so far after Rosie's warning. As for my being unprincipled, I suppose in some respects I can be, but no more than the next man. When I want something badly there isn't anything I won't do to get it. All is fair, Miranda,' he reminded her, and the calm indolence of his voice seemed to underline the steely determination which she knew was his. A strange cold fear began to grow in her mind, crowding out the anger and making her wish that she was anywhere but in that shadowy, seductive room alone with him.

He stepped towards her, both hands outstretched, smiling in the way he had smiled at her when they had first met.

'Come, Miranda, let's take hands. I haven't done anything very wrong, only provided you with shelter when you had none and kept some rather unpleasant information to myself. Perhaps I shouldn't have read your letter, but I was concerned when I saw how far you had swum, knowing that you aren't a really strong swimmer. Won't you forgive me?'

As he approached she backed away, afraid to forgive him in case he used his undeniably attractive physical presence to overwhelm her.

'Stay away from me,' she stammered. 'Don't you dare touch me!'

'You should know better than to say "don't dare" to me,' he chided her, half laughing, as he came closer. 'Forbidden

173

fruit is always the most tempting. But you don't have to be loyal to Joe any more, so why not kiss and be friends, Miranda?'

She was tempted to do what he suggested, but fear held her back: fear that he was playing at a favourite pastime and she was the nearest woman available. She backed away, hoping she was backing towards the door, but she had misjudged the direction and was brought up short against the velvet-covered sofa. The edge caught her behind the knees and she sank down abruptly on to its softness. Before she could stand up again he was beside her, one hand encircling her wrist lightly, his thigh hard against hers, his bare shoulder leaning close to hers.

'Do you remember a shack, Miranda, and an old straw bed in a corner?' he murmured close to her ear, and she could smell the tang of the sea on his skin. 'Do you remember a storm-rent beach and water swirling round our feet? Do you remember walking beside the sea under the stars on the island of flowers?'

She twisted her head to the side in an attempt to avoid his mouth for whose touch she had secretly longed during the interminable tropical nights in the bridal chamber upstairs.

'No, I don't remember,' she gasped defensively.

'Of course you remember. How could you forget?' he murmured teasingly.

'I can forget that sort of happening as easily as you can,' she retorted. Now she was afraid that her own wayward senses would betray her, causing her to surrender to him. 'There's nothing you can do to make me remember,' she added defiantly.

'Oh, isn't there?' he scoffed, and kissed her just below the ear. Immediately she moved sharply as if stung, throwing her head back out of his reach, and she felt his hand tighten on her wrist.

'No, there isn't. I don't want your kisses. They mean nothing. Keep them for other women, the sort who don't mind being a gallant's fancy!' she cried out, her fear of herself making her strike out to hurt him.

An ugly silence followed her outburst. Warily she looked at him. In the amber glow of the light his face looked as if it had been cast in bronze, reminding her of the dream she had experienced after he had rescued her. His eyes were closed and there was a deep cleft between his eyebrows as if he were in pain.

He opened his eyes suddenly and she flinched away from their expression. Anger was glinting in them, rapier-sharp.

'I'm going to make you pay for that, in a way you'll never forget,' he threatened.

Miranda lunged away from the sofa, but his hand tightened like a manacle. He pulled her back and he wasn't gentle any more. He flung her against the arm of the sofa. Her hair spilled like silk across her face. He kissed her first through that silken screen, then wrenched it away so that he could kiss her more effectively.

Time passed in the shadowy room unnoticed by the two on the sofa, who were swept into another timeless world by the passion which flared unexpectedly between them.

A door opened. A slight figure appeared in the opening, head bent, listening.

'Roger? Are you there? Yes, you are. I can hear you breathing. Is someone with you?'

Moving slowly and reluctantly, Roger let his mouth slide along Miranda's cheek in a lingering caress, while he caught his breath and steadied it, before sitting up. Miranda raised heavy eyelids, saw the curve of his cheek, the glimmer of an eye, and then he had gone, rising to his feet. Without the warmth of him pressed close against her she felt cold.

'I'm here, Marnie,' he said calmly. 'So is Miranda.'

'Oh, I'm glad. She was upset because she thought she'd been tricked into staying with us. I didn't want her to feel like that. I was afraid.' Marnie's voice rose slightly and she put her hands to her face, pressing her fingers against her eyes. 'I was afraid I'd gone and said something wrong again. Everything is all right, isn't it, Roger?'

He went over to her and put his arms around her. She buried her head against his shoulder.

'Everything is all right,' he comforted her. 'There's no need to be afraid. You've never done anything wrong.'

'Yes, I have,' she asserted. 'I shouldn't have said anything to Josephine. I was a silly prig. I should have been like the monkeys, seen no evil, heard no evil and spoken no evil, because there wasn't any evil in her or in you, was there?'

'No, there wasn't. It was a mistake for which we both paid, Marnie,' he said gently. 'I wish I'd never met Josephine, let alone been tempted to kiss her, but she belongs to the past now and has no part of our future. Let's forget her, shall we?'

'Oh, I'll be glad to forget, if you will,' replied Marnie fervently. 'Miranda says she wants to go home. She doesn't want to stay here any longer. Are you going to let her go?'

He laughed and gave her a little shake before moving away from her back to the table.

'If she wants to go how can I make her stay? Do you really think I could behave like one of our piratical ancestors and keep her here against her will?' he queried mockingly, as he sent Miranda a bright cold glance. She was standing beside the sofa trying to smooth her hair into place with her hands, feeling glad that Marnie could not see her dishevelled state.

'When would you like to leave, Miranda?' he asked, and to Marnie he must have sounded casually polite.

'Tomorrow, if that's possible,' she said, trying to match the cool evenness of his voice and failing because she had realised suddenly what leaving Fortuga would mean.

'It can be arranged quite easily,' he replied. 'And now if you'll both excuse me I'd like to finish this score before dinner.'

'Of course,' murmured Miranda. Then, seeing bewilderment and distress clouding Marnie's face, she hastened to go to her and putting an arm through hers, suggested that they walked in the garden until dinner was ready, and guided her from the room before she could ask her brother any more awkward questions.

CHAPTER SEVEN

The mad March wind danced along the street whipping wickedly at girls' skirts, tossing paper into the air. It whistled of the grey wastes of the North Sea, of seagulls and fishing smacks, of daffodils and springtime.

Miranda bent her head to its prankish volatile ways as she hurried home from the station one Friday evening, and thought of another kind of wind which blew steadily and consistently across bright blue sea, making it dance and glitter, and which lifted the heavy broad leaves of palm trees as they shadowed beaches of bone-white sand.

It all seemed like a dream, that cruise through the islands and the short stay on the island of Fortuga; a dream she would never forget, yet it was over a month since she had left Gallant's Fancy and had flown in a small aeroplane over the dancing sea to Grenada and from there to Antigua, looking down at the islands of the wind which had seemed like so many stars flung carelessly in the sea.

From Antigua she had flown to San Juan and had been able to catch a plane for London so easily that she had felt, quite irrationally, that it was unfair of the islands to let her leave them with such little fuss, not bothering to detain her in any way, just as Roger had let her go, knowing that she would never forget him.

But Marnie hadn't let her go easily. Poor blind Marnie had been upset and her sightless eyes had filled with tears as she had said goodbye.

'There's something wrong, isn't there?' she had persisted. 'Something has gone wrong between you and Roger. I can feel it—a sense of rejection.'

Wary of that instinctive sense of Marnie's, Miranda had mumbled something about her hostess having been mistaken and had escaped from further questions when the car had arrived in front of the house and James Williams had appeared to take her suitcases. She had kissed Marnie hurriedly and had fled. Roger had not come to bid her farewell. In fact she had not seen him since she had left the music room the previous night, and she had been glad that he had kept out of sight.

Now, walking along the familiar road lined with semi-detached houses, she knew why Marnie had used the word rejection. She had rejected Roger when he had wanted to kiss and be friends, and he had rejected her when he had told Marnie he had no wish to keep her on Fortuga after making sure that she would never forget him.

She had returned home to England to take up the threads of her life there, but there had been no threads to take up. Joe had married Dottie and Transmarine had no further use for her services. There had only been Aunt Clara, sitting and listening to her account of all that had happened and saying quite irrelevantly at the end of the account:

'There's more of your mother in you than I'd thought, Miranda. You've fallen in love with this Roger person, haven't you?'

Miranda had denied that any such thing had happened, but Aunt Clara had interrupted her and had said in her usual forthright way:

'Rubbish, of course you have. And the sooner you admit it to yourself instead of fighting it the better you'll feel.'

There didn't seem much point in admitting it when Roger was thousands of miles away, but Miranda did in the privacy of her own bedroom, and shed a few tears about it. She had fallen in love with a man who was serious only about music. Not only was she in love, but she loved him; loved everything about him. Yet she had rejected him. Why? Because she had been afraid he had regarded her as only a passing fancy, and she wanted to be more than that. She wanted to be not only his mistress but his wife, to live with him for ever, sharing joys and sorrows.

Fortunately it had been easy for her to find another job in

179

the neighbouring town of Gravesend. It was not such a potentially exciting job as the one she had had at Transmarine, being only in the small office of a local construction company, but she hoped that new faces and a different route to travel every day would help her forget the cruise and its consequences. She had visited Dottie and Joe in their new detached house and had noted their relief when she had greeted them calmly and had given them a wedding present. Looking at Joe sitting so complacently beside Dottie she had wondered in surprise how she had believed she had been in love with him. He was pleasant enough, but there was no mystery about him, no excitement, at least not for her.

But her hopes that she would eventually forget were doomed to failure. She couldn't forget, and going to bed became an agony because once she had turned off the light and the room was in darkness, the soft tropical night was around her and she was walking beside the shimmering starlit sea, holding hands with Roger.

The wind pulled at her hair and she ran the last few yards down the road to the comparative safety of Aunt Clara's house. At least her aunt was the same as ever, strict, sometimes astringently witty, always complaining about the behaviour of the teenagers she taught, as she had complained for fifteen years, to Miranda's knowledge. She would be in the kitchen now, preparing the evening meal, and as soon as Miranda entered she would probably start telling a story about how badly her Friday afternoon English classes had behaved as they had found double meanings in one of Shakespeare's plays and had spent their time giggling, or had failed to understand some profound thought behind Shelley's beautiful poetry.

Miranda opened the front door and stepped into the lemon-scented umbrella-damp hallway. The tinkly, slightly flat sound of Aunt Clara's upright piano being played caused her to stand, still and amazed, by the closed door. The melody was familiar, expressing youthful innocence with a hint of throbbing passion beneath the innocence. The piano stopped and she heard Aunt Clara speaking. A voice answered. It was masculine and had an indolent lilt to it.

Miranda's fingers groped for the buttons on her coat, found them and undid them. Slowly she slipped the coat off and hung it in the old-fashioned clothes stand. She glanced in the small mirror which was part of the stand. Her face was reflected back, thinner than it used to be, less childish, the eyes slightly shadowed, the cheeks rather pale.

'Is that you, Miranda?' Aunt Clara's bell-like voice pealed out from the sitting room. 'We're in here, by the fire.'

We. There was someone in there after all. She hadn't imagined the sound of the piano or the voice. She walked into the sitting room, a slim composed-looking girl with smooth dark hair, grey eyes, and cheeks which were only faintly pink; a quiet girl who would be nice to come home to any time of the day.

Aunt Clara was sitting in her favourite chair. She was looking very pleased with life and was talking animatedly about music, which was her greatest love after English literature. She was talking to a young man who was sitting on the piano stool with his hands under his thighs. His hair had the glossy sheen of the skin of a chestnut and it lapped the collar of his exquisitely tailored English suit. His handsome aquiline face had been tanned by a stronger sun than that which ever shone in England and his eyes shimmered with a greenish light as he turned and smiled at Miranda.

He stood up and held out his hand. She took it in hers, feeling the vibrant warmth of his grasp against her cool palm. Never had she felt so glad to see anyone. Never had she found a simple handshake such an inadequate form of greeting. She longed to express her joy by flinging her arms around him and kissing him, but Aunt Clara was there, looking on, approving no doubt of the reticent handshake.

'Why are you here?' Miranda asked Roger, once they

had shaken hands. She sat in the chair opposite to Aunt Clara and he sat on the piano stool again.

'Here in England or here in this house?' he parried.

'Here in this house.'

'To see you. I also wanted to make the acquaintance of Aunt Clara.'

He smiled at her aunt, who smiled back with obvious liking.

'Roger and I have been having a most interesting talk about *The Tempest*. He's been composing the music for a new ballet to be performed in London in the autumn. That's why he's come to England. He'll be staying for several months,' boomed Aunt Clara. 'Where did you say you have a flat, Roger?'

Miranda did not hear his reply because she was remembering him saying: *We could meet in London. I have a flat there.*

And here they were meeting, not in a smart apartment, but in Aunt Clara's shabby sitting room.

Roger's glance met hers for a split second and he smiled at her again, not enigmatically or with subtle invitation, but shyly as if he was unsure of her and of her reaction to his presence there. Roger unsure and diffident! She must be imagining it.

'I thought you and your aunt would like to come and have dinner with me this evening,' he said politely.

'Take Miranda,' said Aunt Clara without hesitation. 'She doesn't go out enough. I've an evening class to attend.'

Miranda stared at her aunt in amazement, knowing that she did not have an evening class on a Friday. Aunt Clara telling a barefaced lie and actually winking at her!

'Go and change now, Miranda,' she said forcibly. 'Put on your prettiest dress while I tell Roger where he should take you to have dinner.'

Upstairs it was difficult to decide what to wear because her mind was in a turmoil. In the end she put on the dark blue skirt and frilly white blouse as the only evening clothes

182

she had which were suitable for a wild and windy night in March. Strange little shivers shook her as she recalled the last time she had worn them at Gallant's Fancy. Dared she go out with Roger? Would he bring her back home after dinner or would he kidnap her and take her to his flat? She would feel much safer if Aunt Clara was going with them.

'Safety, Miranda?' she scoffed at herself. 'You threw safety out of the door when you allowed Roger Gallant to persuade you to ride with him in a taxi-cab in San Juan. From then on you were never safe from his piratical ways, and you won't be safe tonight or any other night when he's near you.'

He had hired a car. It was parked outside the house, but she had been too absorbed in thought to notice it when she had arrived home. She sat beside him and watched the headlights lighting up the winding road which delved into the Kentish countryside, on the way to the inn which Aunt Clara had recommended.

They were both silent and Miranda could feel the tension mounting between them. She searched for a way to snap it. When at last she decided to speak Roger spoke too.

'How is Marnie?' asked Miranda.

'Marnie said I was to thank you for the letter you sent to her,' said Roger.

They both laughed and were at ease with each other at last.

'Marnie is well,' replied Roger. 'She and Aubrey have announced their engagement. They'll be married at the end of June. She would like you to be at the wedding and sent an invitation with me. Will you go?'

She felt suddenly very confused.

'I'm very glad for them both. But how can I go? It's a long way to Fortuga. I can't afford the fare. I couldn't get time off to go. I had to find a new job, and it isn't easy to ask for time off when you've only been working for a company for a month.'

Words were pouring out of her, a babbling torrent over

which she had no control. The car slowed down and was swung off the road into a lay-by. The engine was switched off and the lights were turned out. Darkness swirled about them, not the warm velvet darkness of the tropics but the boisterous buffeting dark of the English countryside in March.

'Stop it, Miranda,' ordered Roger crisply. He grasped a tress of her hair and pulled it hard. The pain of the pulling had the effect of making her gasp. Realising she had been babbling almost hysterically, she gulped air and was quiet, then sat shaking as the reaction to seeing him unexpectedly caught up in her.

His grasp on her hair slackened, he put an arm round her shoulders and drew her gently against him. Still shaking, she lay there until the warmth of his body penetrated to her and she felt comforted.

'Has it been bad for you, this past month?' he asked softly.

'Yes.'

'For me, too. I've gone through hell wishing I'd never let you leave Fortuga,' he murmured, and she raised her head to peer at him incredulously, but she could see nothing in the dark. 'That's why I'm here, Miranda. Will you go to Marnie's wedding as my wife?'

She raised a hand to touch his face to make sure she wasn't having a dream. He caught her hand and pressed his lips to the palm of it, then closed her fingers over his kiss.

'I was just making sure that you're really here,' she whispered.

'I'm here all right, a hundred and sixty-five pounds of me,' he answered drily. 'Well? What's your answer?'

'Are you asking me to be your wife because you can't get what you want any other way?' she asked, suspicion forming in her mind again.

The silence reminded her of that dreadful silence in the music room and she hastened to explain herself.

'I'm sorry, Roger,' she said in a small humble voice, 'but

I have to know. You see, marriage is a very serious business for me and ...'

'What the hell do you think it is for me?' he interrupted roughly. 'Why do you think I haven't married before? Simply because until I met you I hadn't met any woman I wanted to live with for the rest of my life. If I didn't love you more than anyone else in the world I'd never forgive you for what you've just said. If I didn't love you, Miranda, I wouldn't be here in this damned draughty car holding you like this.'

Sincerity rang through his voice, making her realise how much she had wronged him.

'I didn't know,' she cried. 'How could I know? Everything I'd heard about you, everything I knew about you was against you. I wanted to love you, but I was afraid that it might be only a temporary attraction for both of us, the result of too much tropical sun.'

'The aphrodisiac effect of a climate which requires the minimum of clothing,' he murmured, then gave a little laugh. 'And to think I warned you about that sort of thing happening when I told you that physical attraction could flare between two people quickly. Then I've only myself to blame for your coolness. But it wasn't like that for me. I *liked* you from the first time I saw you, as you watched the people go by at San Juan airport. I made up my mind to get to know you and find out where you were going.'

'Oh! Then you stood behind me deliberately so that I would step on your foot?' she accused.

'I did, and my little trick worked. I admit I was surprised when I learned that you were going on the same cruise as myself, but it only convinced me that we were meant to meet and know each other, and I stayed with the cruise so that I could see more of you, only to discover that you intended to marry Joe. So I decided to keep my distance, thinking we could just be friends.'

'A "mornings only" friendship,' suggested Miranda teasingly, and he laughed.

'How right you are! It was safer in the morning as we were to find out,' he replied. 'Then Dawn started to show an interest in me. I played along more out of a long-time habit to annoy Thomas than anything else. But it was my turn to become suspicious, and that evening, when you were missing, I offered to go and look for you with the intention of finding out from you whether Ingram was behind Dawn's attempts at seduction. I thought I could kiss you and get away with it. I was wrong. I fell in love with you that evening and knew from the way you responded to my kiss that you weren't in love with Joe, but that you might be half in love with me.'

'Such arrogance!' murmured Miranda, and had her hair pulled by way of retaliation.

'A lot of good knowing that did me,' he remarked drily. 'Just my bad luck, I thought, to fall in love with a girl who was determined to marry someone who had never made love to her, a girl who had been brought up to distrust her own instinctive impulses and who had been pumped full of suspicions of me by her boss.'

'I wasn't suspicious of you at first,' she defended herself. 'I liked you too and enjoyed every morning I spent with you, but when you spent so much time with Dawn it was difficult not to believe the worst of you.'

'I know. I guessed how you were feeling, but time wasn't on my side. I had to do something about stopping Thomas from selling to Ingram, and that meant spending far more time with Dawn than I would have liked. I tried to tell you on the way to Martinique, but you wouldn't listen to me, and I only succeeded in making you more suspicious of me when I suggested that we should meet in London. Later that evening my hopes began to rise again, only to be dashed when you asked me about Josephine. Knowing how suspicious you were about me, I couldn't tell you about her because I doubted very much if you would understand my extremely short, experimental association with her any more than Marnie had understood ten years ago. It seemed

to me then that all I was doing was courting you for Joe. I decided to give up, and chalk up my friendship with you as just another experience, one in which I hadn't called the tune for once.'

'Oh. And I thought you'd lost interest in me because you'd found out I wasn't very exciting after all and that I was only a Girl Friday "dreaming of the day when I was going to marry my dull suburban boy-friend",' she said.

'Who said that?' he asked sharply. 'Doesn't sound like you, Miranda.'

'Dawn. She told me you'd only ever been interested in brief ephemeral affairs with women.'

'And you believed her.' It was his turn to be accusing. 'My few innocuous friendships with the opposite sex, including my acquaintance with Dawn, looked like that because I didn't like any of the women enough to want to live with them,' he said drily. 'I wasn't really sure about you until I found that letter on the beach and learned how you'd been let down; when I saw you nearly drown, because, as I believed then, you'd lost Joe. I realised then how much I loved you and I thought that, given time, I might be able to nullify your suspicions of me. Ingram played into my hands when he said he couldn't wait for you to recover. I kept you at Gallant's Fancy thinking we could travel together to London and that by then you would have realised you loved me. You were responding nicely to treatment, but we still had a long way to go when Marnie, in all innocence, betrayed me and roused all your suspicions again.'

'Why did you let me leave?'

'Would there have been any point in letting you stay?' he countered. 'I was angry with you for daring to belittle my love for you, for thinking that you meant no more to me than any of the other women I'd known. I let you go thinking that when you'd cooled off in the temperate zone you'd find out that it wasn't tropical magic you were suffering from but the real thing, love.'

Miranda was stunned by this revelation of his love for

187

her. She had been so blinded by her own suspicions of him and by her own repressions that she hadn't recognised love when it had come to her, a warm tender feeling which had expressed itself naturally in passionate caresses as well as in sincere concern for her welfare and happiness.

'Oh, how can I show you that I'm sorry for what I suspected, for what I said? What do I have to do or say?' she cried, suddenly overwhelmed by compunction for having doubted him and insulted him.

'Say nothing, but surely you know how to show me. Haven't you learned anything during your short visit to the Caribbean? Haven't I taught you anything? Or are you just an unusually slow learner?'

The mockery was back in his voice, reminding her that he would always be an elusive, tantalising rogue who might not always be so willing to reveal the depths of his feeling for her as he was this evening. Miranda tapped him sharply on one lean cheek to caution him and he caught her hand again.

'Slap me and I'll make you pay for it,' he threatened, and dangerous excitement charged through her, shocking her senses into life.

'Show me how you'll make me pay,' she invited him, throwing back her head, trying to pull away out of reach.

At once she was at the mercy of his marauding kisses until he had reduced her to being a willing captive, incapable of doing anything but responding.

'You haven't given me an answer, Miranda,' he whispered breathlessly in her ear. 'Will you go with me to Marnie's wedding?'

'I'll go anywhere with you, Roger, because I love you,' she replied recklessly.

To her surprise he let her go, switched on the car's engine, turned on the lights and guided the car on to the road facing in the direction from which they had come.

'Where are we going?' she demanded.

'You said you'd go anywhere with me, so I'm taking you

to my flat,' he said smoothly.

'But what about dinner?' she protested. He was kidnapping her after all and there wasn't anything she could do or wanted to do to stop him.

'You shall dine, my love, never fear, in comfort and privacy. I've no intention of courting my betrothed in a car on a public highway or in an eating place in front of strangers. For a few hours we shall be alone and shall learn the language of love together. Then afterwards I'll take you back to Aunt Clara.' He paused, then added with a touch of mischief, 'On second thoughts maybe I won't take you back to her. I'll keep you out all night.'

'Pirate!' she accused, tenderly teasing, and joined in his laughter as they sped through the dark windy night, together at last.

OMNIBUS — The 3 in 1 HARLEQUIN
only $1.50 per volume

HARLEQUIN OMNIBUS

☐ **JEAN S. MacLEOD**

The Wolf Of Heimra (#990)
Summer Island (#1314)
Slave Of The Wind (#1339)
$1.50

☐ **ELEANOR FARNES**

The Red Cliffs (#1335)
The Flight Of The Swan (#1280)
Sister Of The Housemaster (#975)
$1.50

☐ **MARY BURCHELL**

A Home For Joy (#1330)
Ward Of Lucifer (#1165)
The Broken Wing (#1100)
$1.50

☐ **ESSIE SUMMERS**

Bride In Flight (#933)
Meet On My Ground (#1326)
Postscript To Yesterday (#1119)
$1.50

THE 3 IN 1 VOLUME —
EACH VOLUME BY THE SAME AUTHOR
— ONLY $1.50 EACH